The Catalan Key

BOOK THREE OF THE LOST HERITAGE TRILOGY

by Jenny Dee

The Catalan Key

©2020 by Jennifer Dee Communications LLC

Cover Illustrations ©2020 Chelsea Yolalan
Cover Photography ©2020 Anna Subbotina/Depositphotos.com
Artwork ©2020 Andrejs Severetnikovs/Depositphotos.com

ISBN: 978-1-7346295-6-9
Printed in the United States of America

Dedication

To every woman who ever doubted herself; we are all the dark and the light. May we find peace with our flaws and embrace our authenticity.

We are perfect just as we are.

1

"**D**on't stop," I moaned, as the dripping of the hot wax made my chest flinch. I looked into the eyes of my lover, who knew exactly what I needed to feel better.

Knew how when I was feeling angry or insecure, the best thing to do was to fuck it out.

Now, don't go judging me. I'm not like my pretentious, perfect oldest sister, Megan, or my girl scout of a sister, Mia. I never saw how living the "good girl" life was any fun. Besides, someone needed to be the rebel of the family.

It's not like I am necessarily a "bad girl," either. I don't do anything hardcore. I've dabbled with some drugs, but I grew out of that phase, realizing pot was all I needed to soothe my nerves. It was cleaner and quicker than a trip to the beach. I didn't need to chant with my feet in the sand to make life better.

Combine a good high with my love of sex, and it made life super pleasurable. After all, isn't that what we are here for on this planet? To enjoy it?

I fully intend to live life to the fullest until someone has to cart me away in a wooden box. Preferably laced with diamonds.

The way things going, I was on my way to having everything I've ever wanted in life. Soon, I'd be going to Spain to claim my lost heritage and have all the money I could ever need to build my art gallery and buy a beautiful house like both my sisters have.

Looking over to the man who just made me orgasm multiple times over the last four hours (thank you, roomie, for having a business trip!), I also knew I had found the one who finally understood me and accepted me as I was—the flawed, yet gorgeous human being I am.

I have no problem admitting I am hella sexy. I am proud of my exotic, Mediterranean looks, my long, dark jet black hair that loves to be pulled and my luminescent blue eyes that call, 'come hither, my love.'

My body has made the boys swoon my entire life, following after me like a puppy dog begging for a bone. Put on a tight leather dress and stiletto boots that ride my legs like a biker on his hog, and I can pretty much get anyone I want.

But this one—this one actually wants more than that from me. He gives me everything my body craves yet stimulates my mind and heart in ways I never thought possible.

I finally feel supported in my dreams of becoming an artist. I'm not put down over my "choice" of a bartending career as I fight for my rightful place in the creative community. He knows that it takes time and the right opportunity, and with his connections, he's working on getting me more exposure for my recent canvases of Ireland and the ones in my head of Italy I've promised him.

Even though those trips were more about my sisters and their journeys and not mine, I was still inspired by them to go back to my craft. Long hours trying to make ends meet didn't leave much time for sculpting or painting or even doodling; but after witnessing the pure beauty of those Irish landscapes, I couldn't help but be called to capture them with my watercolors.

Those majestic Cliffs of Moher where Megan had her epiphany and remembered who she was; how the curvature of the mountain resembled the profile of an old woman, earning its name as Hag's Head. How there was no beginning nor end to the sunset-layered sky, melting into fiery reds and oranges imprinted in my memory.

Then there was the fascinating, weathered lighthouse at Clare's Island. Just Mia and I took that trip for an absolutely amazing few days at the spa. I made a painting especially for her, knowing she found her serenity in a book, miles away from the challenges of home. I had hoped that it would symbolize lighting her own way, no matter how dark it got.

For Mom and Granny, I recreated an image of our ancestral home, so that they could look at it and feel like they were a part of our journey, even from across the ocean. Within it, I etched the imagery of the ring that Meg received as a family heirloom to make it truly a meaningful, O'Sullivan family painting.

Damn, was that rock stunning, by the way. Green diamond? *Of course, meant for Meg,* I thought sardonically. Whatever. Moving on.

Me—I was so captivated by the art galleries and culture that I ended up sculpting a few smaller pieces of art...a mini Spanish Arch, the Blarney Castle's Witch Stone and a pint of Guinness, which secretly represented my own little love affair in the Emerald Isle, I recalled bashfully to myself. My sisters weren't the only ones to have some fun, you know.

I'm very proud of my work. So much so, that as soon

as this sex marathon is over, I'll get back to creating my Italian inspirations.

I happened to like Florence just a tad bit more than Ireland, though they are both so culturally unique that it would be unfair to compare them. After taking the long, half a day's worth flight back home all by myself, I had more than enough time to start brainstorming sketches of the scenery.

I definitely needed a vineyard painting—a beautiful scene filled with intertwining grapevines in the background, with an elegantly set table with glasses of wine off to the side, and a bin of partially crushed red and purple grapes front and center; maybe with a foot walking towards it to represent our cool, make-your-own-wine stomping experience.

Oh, and somehow I'd love to weave in Mia's expertly carved jewelry box. Or, make that a different painting. To be determined. Wait—I got it—the Bardini Garden with its wisteria tunnel and the box lying on the ground with a simple ray of sunlight that escaped in through the trees to highlight it. Yes, I liked that imagery very much.

Speaking of gardens—wow. All the statues in those beautifully manicured estates—those heavenly white marbled carvings of wildlife and deities joined together in play and protection; they took my breath away.

Not typically much of a gardener, I was suddenly inspired to design a landscape that I would have once I purchased my new home. Mia can help me with the floral arrangements (and maybe keep them alive), but the statues would be of my own creation.

I can hear them now, the visitors…*oh Marissa, these are exquisite! Where did you get these?*

They are one-of-a-kind Rossi originals, I would reply.

I'd be happy to create an inspired piece for your own garden, if you'd like.

Oh, yes please! they'd demand.

I'd perhaps make some for my own art gallery; the one I will open up by the end of this year with good ole Grampy's inheritance (I hope).

Though I will admit that the greatest piece of work that I am inspired to conceive somehow—not sure yet if by paint or clay—will pay homage to the Tree of Love that the Marchesi brothers took us to see in a small, random town, with its intricate branches and symbolic medallions. Now that was something to admire.

Although, I did kind of cringe when they bestowed a blessing of eternal love and luck on me while standing in front of the enchanted tree. At that time, I knew I was falling for the amazing man lying beside me, but given my track record, I'm hesitant to believe anything in my life is meant to last.

I usually end up sabotaging it and pushing people away. But then again, they are usually assholes and when I finally get their number, out the door they go.

But looking over at my love, his naked body glistening from the sweat and indications of fatigue forming around his beautiful emerald green eyes, I knew there was something different about him. He had been there for me through this entire journey, supporting me even when I felt left behind while Meg and Mia had their special adventures.

Why am I always the last one? Does it always have to go in age order?

I know, I do have a little (okay, medium-sized) green monster living inside my head. She's ugly, too. Who could blame me, though? These so-called amazing "sister" trips never turn out as planned. I'm pushed to the side like some tag-along so they can go "find themselves."

And now both my sisters have exactly what they wanted and decided to leave me behind (again) to come back to New York alone. At first, I wondered how they could do that to me, but then I realized it was nothing different from normal.

Well, at least not for Meg, who has always been self-absorbed. It's not that I begrudge her love—I am truly happy she has finally found someone and opened her heart to Kieran. I can't help but really like him and think he is exactly what she needs in a partner to keep her from being so serious all the time.

I just wish her new love and Ireland-inspired transformation would have returned her to the sister who used to remember that I existed and paid a little more attention to my life.

But it's actually Mia who surprised me the most. She always cares about everyone and checks in on me more than anyone else bothers to. I guess she deserves time to think about herself and stay in Italy a few more days, but still. Ugh. I'm not good at doing this alone thing.

The only thing making me feel a little better about all of this is knowing my time is coming two months from now. But I'm not exactly the patient type.

Yes, I'm complicated. I'm up and down with my emotions and opinions. I love and hate equally. I can be extremely impulsive, stubborn and feisty. Sometimes irrational. I think with passion instead of logic.

I can't help it, but looking over again at my hot and sexy boyfriend, I can finally say I hit pay dirt.

Joshua Perkins.

Who knew that the moment he walked through that

door to tell us about some unknown grandfather, that it would be more than an instant attraction? Yeah, I know I've been lying to my family about dating my old roommate, Tony.

As if. He couldn't find my G-spot if his life depended on it.

But Joshua—oh my God!—we clicked like a key in a lock.

At first, I thought he had a pull towards my big sister, but he told me that Meg was way too proper for him. As the youngest in his family, he could relate to that feeling of never being good enough, so he was able to see me for who I really was, and not just my looks—the only thing everyone else seemed to care about.

It started with mind-blowing sex. Jesus, how he was open to my kinky side. Not that I am a crazy sadist, but I didn't mind a little game of bondage, a little light whip or a nipple clamp here and there. He indulged my sexual fluidity by allowing another woman to join us so I could still experience the sweetness of the female touch and taste.

He even didn't mind when I invited another man to devour me while he watched.

Don't worry, I am always safe. I may be sexually adventurous, but I'm not stupid. No man (or woman) will be giving me any kind of disease or getting me knocked up, thank you. Kids were not for me. Not at the moment, anyway. I had a career to jumpstart first and didn't really think I was the settle-down type.

At least, I wasn't until Joshua crossed my path. Now, as I lie here in his arms and think about how he has been there for me all these months and how deep our feelings have grown for each other, I've realized that maybe I could have my own happily ever after, after all.

I've struggled with telling my family about him, even though he's told me from the very beginning that I should just be honest with them; that there is nothing to hide. Unfortunately, my relationships don't tend to last, so I hold off on admitting to being in one until I know there may be a chance it could work.

I also just can't stand the judgment that oozes out of the eyes of my loved ones. Just like when Meg deduced that Tony wasn't my roommate anymore because we slept together. Like she was so virtuous.

I'm not going to get into her private life, but on the outside, she pulls off the perfect lady illusion and enjoys a detached sex life behind the scenes—well, that was before Kieran, anyway. Funny how when we were listening to the story about our wicked ancestral aunt Dominica appearing one way to society, but another way privately, I unfairly matched her to Meg. I know, my sister isn't that bad. I love her. But it doesn't mean I can't stand her sometimes.

Back to me, though. It's frustrating to hide who I am so that I'm not looked down upon all the time. Especially by my "perfectly" behaved family.

I love sex. I don't know why that is such a problem in today's world. Women get such a bad rap for pursuing it and enjoying it, and that's bullshit. Our bodies were made for pleasure just like men, and you don't see them branded with vicious names like slut or whore.

But if that's the label you want to slap on me, go right ahead. I'm still going to do my thing and not apologize for it.

I might have to apologize for keeping Josh a secret, though. Sure, they've been fine with me not saying anything until things got more serious in the past. But I'm not so sure they're going to be okay with me having lied about his identity and making them think it was Tony. Or letting them alternatively think it was my current apartment pal, Jay. After all, he's my best friend and it would have made more sense.

I have my reasons for pretending, though. I really didn't think it would get so—complicatedly real. But I had to cave and reveal my lover's "name" at some point because my caring, yet perceptive sisters could tell I was getting something more than a good roll in the sheets. Apparently, I was glowing.

I didn't mean to lie. It just came out. I knew that Josh's connection to our grandfather's family might hurt Granny's feelings. After all, he is the great nephew of the woman who married our grandfather. After everything she had been through, I wanted to protect her. I didn't want to be the reason she had a heart attack or something; she has already weakened physically since having to relive this experience.

But now I was at a crossroads. I never expected to fall in love with Josh, and I was pretty certain he had deep feelings for me, too. I knew I had to come clean.

Maybe that was part of my new journey—to not be afraid of disappointing my family anymore. To live my life without apologies and have everyone just accept me for who I am. Maybe now that it's my turn, the focus would *finally* be on me and *my* happiness.

"There seems to be a lot going on in that beautiful head of yours," his sultry voice spoke, breaking my deep thoughts. "What's going on?"

"Nothing. Just thinking."

"What about?" He turned so that his glare could burn right through me with kindness and love. I adored how his cat-like eyes sat glowing within his rounded, whiter-than-an-Irishman pale face, with a sharp nose and thin lips that curved into a mischievous smile.

He had a killer body, made possible by his gym addiction and perhaps acrobatic-like sexual performances. His arms were solid, as was his six-pack. And I was certainly not unhappy to see the package waiting underneath his boxers for me the moment our clothes first hit the floor.

This man was fucking fine. And, he genuinely cared about my feelings, making him even sexier to me. He was so easy to open up to. It was a bonus that he came into this situation already knowing about the heritage journey, so he was instantly protective from the beginning.

Plus, he never once probed; he always respected my grandfather's request that the contents of the letters remained a secret. Whenever I wanted to share, he would stop me and say that he couldn't betray his professional oath—even if he was curious. I really respected that about him.

Trust has never been easy for me, but I found myself able to share whatever was in my heart so easily with Josh, knowing that he would never judge me.

"Pretty much everything, I guess. How my sisters are still off gallivanting through Europe while they left me on my own to come back here to nothing."

"So, I'm nothing now," he teased, faking a stab to the heart.

"No, silly. That's not what I meant," I said as I gave him a light pull of his dirty blonde, messy head of tousled hair. "You know exactly what I mean. They are off in their brand new rich lives after having wonderful, meaningful adventures and I'm just stuck here waiting for my turn."

"Your turn is coming, my love. Spain is only two months away. Then it will be all about you, just like you like it," he joked.

I ignored his mocking. I was trying to be serious. Wisely, he caught on and stopped kidding around.

"Marissa, just have a little patience. If your journey is anything like your sisters', then you are in for one hell of a ride. Enjoy the moment, babe. Don't rush through it."

"You're right, I guess. I just hope that it will be as amazing for me as it was for them."

"It will be. I promise."

"How can you promise something like that?"

"Because I see your heart, and I know what you deserve. Your grandfather orchestrated this so that each one of you had a special heirloom—and an awakening to come. He never met you face to face, but it seemed as though he did a psychically flawless job of understanding exactly what your sisters needed and represented; I have no doubt he knows the same for you."

His perspective was always insightful…and usually on target. Damn it, I hate a man who's right all the time.

"Thank you for saying that," I responded, before my mind wandered off again to the clouds.

"Now where did you go? Come on. Talk to me," he urged, gently stroking back a loose tendril of hair from my face.

"I—I just wonder what's in store for me. You said that my grandfather would know what I needed, but that's just the thing. What is it? Meg's journey was about love— isn't that something, as a single woman at the time, he would wish for me to have?

"But then Mia's journey was about following her dreams—yet again, isn't that what I have been struggling to do for years? If it's not love or success for me, then what is it?" I couldn't help but ramble on now that the emotional flood gates had opened.

"Meg has always been the smart, ambitious one. She has gotten everything she's ever wanted in her life. Granted, she's worked hard for it—but even the moment she wished for real love, *poof!* Her wish was the universe's command—or rather, some Blarney witch's spell manifested.

"And Mia has always been the kind, good-hearted sister who people adore, and now that she wants to pursue her childhood vision of opening a restaurant, no one questions her and we're all supposed to be completely on board to help in any way we can. I can't help but feel like it won't be the same for me.

"I've always been the impulsive, black sheep of my family. I know they love me, and I don't doubt it for a second. But it's always Meg with her condescending 'wow, that was actually a deep thought' shit and Mia with her patronizing 'one day it will happen' crap that gets me.

"I don't want to wait anymore, Josh. I don't want to live beneath their expectations—or mine. I am smarter than they give me credit for, kinder than they see and more determined than ever to get exactly what I want."

"And what is it that you want?" I thought long and hard before answering that one.

"Respect. And I'm tired of trying to earn it."

"Well, you already have mine," he smiled as he looked at me, running a finger down my reddened cheek.

"I see who you are, Marissa. I see the brilliance. I see the hard work ethic and the passion behind your recent artwork—they are outstanding and full of life and emotion. You have a golden heart that has sucked me in without warning.

"I love you."

I did not see that coming. I mean, I felt it, at least on my side, but I didn't know that he would actually return my feelings. Suddenly, I felt extremely uncomfortable and started to rise from the bed. He gently stopped me and pulled me back down so that our naked bodies were warm against each other—but it was a different warmth than sexual afterglow.

"Did you hear what I just said?"

"Yes," I squeaked out.

"I love you with every ounce of my soul. I knew it from the moment I laid eyes on you. And not just your smoking body, which I am very much fond of," he added seductively before turning back to genuine.

"I love every part of you. The woman inside—the insecure one, the fiery one—even the bitchy one. But most especially, the one who takes me as I am, listens to me and makes me feel like there is no other man in the world." He hesitated, looking down, almost afraid to make eye contact for a moment.

"Am I alone in this feeling?" he finally asked, before raising his head up once again to look into my deer-in-a-headlight spooked eyes.

He let me take a few moments to catch my breath and formulate a response. Usually, I can drop the "L" bomb like no big deal even after a few weeks; it was so easy for me to fall in and out of love. But this man—this man right here had changed the game on me.

I really, truly, sincerely, without a doubt, love him. And that scares the shit out of me. Because this time—

this time when I say it, my heart means it.

"These last few months have been absolutely amazing, in so many ways. No one has ever been as supportive and on my side as you have—without judgment, without chiding me, without ever making me feel less.

"You've inspired me, challenged me and accepted me for everything that I am, the good and the bad. You don't know how much you being here has meant to me. I've never experienced anything like this before.

"I do love you; I love you, Joshua Perkins, with every cell of my being."

He then leaned in for a slow burning kiss, one that was not of rushed or dramatic lust; but of a gentle, soul-deepening, heart-melting connection. We then made love—*love*—in a way that I had never experienced with a man before.

It was then that I decided the charade was up. I loved this man, and he loved me, and it was time to stop living in the shadows.

2

With Meg still out of town and Mia sick from traveling, both unable to attend for what would typically be our traditional Sunday family dinner, I thought it was the perfect way to break the news gently to Mom and Granny first—instead of to a whole crowd of watchful eyes.

I decided I would announce that I was seeing (and in love with) Josh, and that he would be joining us for dessert so they could get to know him better. By the end of this evening, my secret would be out, and I could finally live life in the open.

But first, I had to get through this day. I had hours before dinner, and my mind was racing through all of the different scenarios. Would they accept him with big, warm Granny hugs? Would they go into inquisition mode? Would they be happy for me or tell me I was crazy? Oh God, make it five o'clock already so I can get this over with.

I had to find something to do to pass the time, so I started baking. Now, Mia was a chef extraordinaire in the kitchen but baking—that was my jam. No one came close to my confectionery delights; I was in high demand around the holidays for my scratch-made cookies, cakes and pies.

But what to make for Sunday dessert in the summer? Oh, I know—they love my fresh fruit tarts. I'll make mini portions and fill them with different favorite fruits. Raspberries for Granny, banana cream for Mom and a tropical mango for Bruce, my mom's new boyfriend.

I liked Bruce well enough, but he was another one who always seemed to be questioning me as a human being. He was kind, funny and polite. Yet something was off; I couldn't put my finger on it, but there was this vibe about him that made me edgy.

No use in telling Mom about this though. She was head over heels for this man, and I am the last person on earth who would want to take her happiness away— especially since it took her years before she could even look at a man after Daddy died. No, I would have to trust her judgment and hope that he really was the good person she claimed he was. Even though I think at heart, she is way too innocent a person to be an intuitive judge of character—especially with men. Time will tell, I guess.

I secretly wished he would not be there tonight so that I could talk with Mom and Granny alone, but maybe it wouldn't hurt to have another male body around as I introduced Josh to the tigresses. He could help run interference—I was pretty sure I could at least count on him for that. You know, male solidarity and all.

While kneading the dough for the crusts, I realized my unfocused anxiety was shredding my delicate tart bases and I had to start over. Maybe using a rolling pin wasn't such a good idea. I thought blondies might be safer, so I was happy to find some white chocolate chips in the cabinet. *Good, I don't have to make a store run—* my decision was made.

While the blondies were cooling, I began pacing again, trying to find the right words to use tonight. Why was this so difficult? Why couldn't I just come out and say it? Since when was I shy about telling anyone what was on my mind?

Because I loved him. Because it was real. Because I never brought home a man to my family I believed was "the one" who would last. For once, I was really frightened over whether or not I would get their approval. I think I just bit my last decent nail off.

Turns out, I had nothing to worry about. Seated at my grandmother's Lenox-set kitchen table, dining on her famous meatloaf, the words just naturally came to me when they asked what was new in my world.

"Joshua Perkins? You mean that lawyer who read us my father's will?" asked Mom incredulously.

"Yes," I said sheepishly. "I wanted to tell you earlier, but I was afraid to hurt Granny's feelings, since he, well, you know—is Julia's family."

"Oh my darling, Marissa," Granny began, looking at me with her pretty blue eyes that matched her pants suit. "I wish you didn't keep this a burden all to yourself. You poor thing. All this time, worrying about *me* and wondering if I would be okay with it?"

I looked at her with rare tears in my eyes and simply nodded my head.

"My beautiful girl, you do not know me very well at all," she advised with a kind smile. "I would never judge a man based on who his family was. If that were the case, then you would never exist, now would you?"

She made a valid point. The Marinos were assholes, and yet she fell deeply in love with my grandfather. He turned out to be an asshole as well, but at least he was a good enough man to admit it in the end.

"Besides, I never had a problem with Julia herself," she explained. "I never met the woman, obviously, but I do remember Leigh telling me about her when we ran away to get married. He felt bad about leaving the woman he was betrothed to behind with the society of wolves, saying she was quite a lovely and nice person.

"And when Joshua was here—under attack from all of us, I might add—he held his own, and was very sympathetic and patient as we grieved and learned all about Leigh's plan. I would very much like to meet him under different circumstances and get to know the man who has stolen our girl's heart."

"I agree, sweetheart," added Mom. "It brings me such joy to see a sparkle in your eyes and love in your heart. We should have him join us next week for dinner."

"Well," I began, "I already invited him for dessert tonight. I hope that's okay. He'll be here in about an hour."

They both looked at each other and smiled. "Perfect. We can't wait."

I was so relieved that they were supportive instead of angry with me. This was going to be a great night after all—I think. But I noticed Bruce sitting back in his chair, tall, dark and sophisticated like the lawyer type that he is (yet much more stuffy than my Josh) with an air of disapproval on his boy-next-door face.

I wanted to ask, *What's wrong, Bruce? Sad that you are no longer the only Alpha male of the group?* But my Mom, who must have noticed his distance herself, beat me to it.

"You're awfully quiet, my dear. What's wrong?" He managed a fake grin as he looked into her eyes to respond.

"Nothing at all. You were having a family discussion. It's not my place to butt in," he said, but then turned to my direction. "Not that it is my business, but I think it is wonderful that you have found someone that makes you so happy."

If he had a bridge to sell, I wasn't about to buy it. Did my Mom and Granny really fall for his faux blessing? Not wanting to let this jackass ruin my good mood, I excused myself so I could call Josh to let him know the good news—that they were waiting to welcome him with open arms.

It was a delightful evening. Everyone—including stodgy Bruce—managed to interact swimmingly and all get along. Although I noticed a few awkward exchanges between the men, for the most part, it was easygoing and lighthearted. I couldn't have asked for a better night.

As we were getting ready to leave, Mom pulled me over to the side.

"I am glad you finally told us, baby girl. None of us really believed it was Tony," she hinted.

"You didn't?" She just laughed her 'you can't get anything past your mom' laugh.

"Not for a second," she replied. "But I did think it might have been Jay, so you got me there. I knew you would tell us when you were ready. As long as he makes you happy, I am thrilled for you, my sweet daughter."

"I am really happy, Mom. I've never felt like this before. It's kinda crazy."

"Good. It's supposed to be a crazy adventure, this love thing. Have you told your sisters?"

"Not yet." Even though I knew deep down they would support me, I couldn't help but fear the inevitable taunting.

"Well, next week, Meg will be calling in for dinner and we can leave you and Mia to speak with her alone before we all join around the table. I'd expect that you'd want to bring Josh every week?"

"I haven't thought that far ahead, Mom. I can't—if I do, I'm afraid this will all blow up in my face."

"Oh my girl, if there is one thing you must learn, it is that you deserve the happiness in front of you, and that it can last. Don't be so caught up in fear that you push joy away," she warned. I looked at her with my little girl eyes full of terror and nodded in consent. I was so not comfortable in this unchartered territory called love.

"It will all be okay," she soothed as she drew me in for a big mama bear hug. God, how I loved this woman.

"That went surprisingly well," Josh said as we sat in the car in front of my apartment.

"I know," I replied. "I didn't expect that."

"I really like your grandmother. She's hysterical."

"Yeah. She seemed to like you, too. I can tell," I beamed.

"Not sure about your mom's boyfriend, though," he noted.

"I noticed you giving each other looks all evening. Do you know him?"

"Not quite. Our firms cross paths on occasion, so I know of his reputation. Excellent criminal lawyer, from what I hear. We sometimes get involved behind the scenes when contested wills or nasty divorce settlements come into play."

"Oh." He was hiding something. I could tell from the way he shifted his eyes uncomfortably.

"What?" he asked as I stared him down.

"Why do I feel like there's more to this story?" He hesitated, huffing out a huge breath of frustration.

"Listen, Mar, I just met your family. I don't want to cause any problems."

"If there is something I should know, then spill it. We promised to always tell it to each other straight, remember?"

"Okay. But promise me you won't go storming off in a fit of rage when I tell you."

"I wouldn't—okay, I promise," having to swear an oath because he was right. I might be a little bit of a hothead.

"I've never met Bruce personally, but I have heard of him. Rumors only, though. Nothing verifiable."

"Rumors about what?" I nudged.

"I don't know how to tell you this," he started off, procrastinating all the way. I sat cross-armed in the car staring him down like a drill sergeant, waiting for him to stop being so damn theatrical about it and just tell me already.

"His now ex-wife had brought him up on charges of physical assault, which led to their divorce. His name was cleared, but whenever you hear a story like that, it makes you wonder if he is guilty and used his connections to get off, or if he really is innocent."

I just sat there, the pissy-ness growing instead me like an oak tree from an acorn. The anger was mighty and he knew me well—I was about to explode. I *knew* something was off about him. If that man even *thinks* of laying a hand on my mother…

"Babe, I didn't tell you to upset you. You asked. I just met your mom and she seems really nice—and vulnerable. He could very well be harmless. But if I kept quiet and something happened to her, I would never forgive myself."

I started to come down from a boil to a simmer. Just his presence was the soothing force I needed in my life to bring me rationality before impulse. Plus, the fact that he was wearing a green polo shirt that matched those crazy intense eyes of his didn't hurt to distract me from my semi-murderous thoughts.

"How credible are your sources?" I asked in a monotonous, no feeling tone.

"It's an actual case. Public record. No evidence to support her claims, though, which is why it was dismissed. She could have been after his money and made it up. Don't rush to conclusions," he advised.

"All I am saying is to watch your mom for any signs of distress and to monitor him for any signs of a suppressed personality. I'm sure she can handle herself. She doesn't seem like the insecure type to be with a man who would abuse her in any way."

He made a valid argument there. My mother wasn't one to allow any monkey business; the first sign of anything off and she'd be out of there. Naïve or not, of that, I was certain.

I decided I would just catalogue this nugget of information in the recesses of my brain and keep a close watch on this Bruce guy. I'll give him the benefit of the doubt for now—but one wrong move, and that man will wish he never crossed my path.

The next Sunday, Mia and I arrived earlier to video chat with Meg and Kieran before Josh and Bruce arrived for dinner. We were having it at Mom and Granny's again because the kids caught Mia's cold and her house was festering with germs. And my apartment was out of the question because Jay already had plans for friends to come over to watch a baseball game.

I told them about Josh, and they were much more encouraging and excited for me than I expected. In fact, I was waiting for Meg's chiding about how she thought she would be the one to land him first, or joke that he was just the next victim in a long line of broken hearts, but she surprised me by saying she noticed the immediate chemistry and was genuinely thrilled that I was in love.

Mia was a little more cautious, with her motherly and ex-wife of a cop questions, but I think I answered them all to her satisfaction as she enveloped me in a big sister hug. I can't even begin to describe the weight that has finally been lifted off my shoulders. I should have never doubted my family's love and support for me. Sometimes I really do think I have them built up in my head all wrong.

As Mia was setting the dining room table with Granny, and I helped Mom place the pot roast into serving dishes in the kitchen, I thought it was the ideal time to check in on her before the men showed up.

"So, how are things going with Bruce?"

"Very well," she beamed. She looked exceptionally pretty today in a mauve-colored sundress with harmonizing sandals—even her fingers and toes matched. I loved how her style was always so complementary and precise.

"I really like him, Mar. He is so thoughtful. The other day I mentioned that I had a little pink parasol as a child for whenever I was out in the sun, and next thing you know, I had one in my hands before he took me on a sunset stroll," she said dreamily.

"That's sweet. So…he's good to you?" I investigated, not so subtly. She was visibly taken aback by my detective-like tone, jerking up to a straightened back, defensive position.

"Yes, very good. He is one of the kindest, most gentle men I've ever known—aside from Daddy. Why are you asking me this?"

"Well, Mom, you can never be too careful these days," I alluded. But she's a smart cookie. She knew exactly what I was talking about, and somehow, I was reassured by that.

"I assume you heard about his ex-wife's allegations?" she said, turning back to wipe off some of the gravy drippings that fell onto the counter with double annoyance.

"Yes, but only because Josh thought we should know," I defended. "He didn't want to cause trouble, but he thought it wouldn't be right if he kept the information to himself. He didn't want anything bad to happen to you in case the rumors were actually true."

"Honey, I'm not mad at Josh," she said, cooling down her almost-temper at having to defend the man she loved. "I think it's sweet how he looks out for you and was worried about me. It's endearing. But neither of you have anything to worry about."

"Are you sure?"

"Yes, baby. Bruce was upfront with me about it from the beginning and we have had long talks. The allegations were just that—he never laid a finger on Eleanor. And I believe that. He has never given me any indication he is capable of violence, ever."

"That's good to hear," I exhaled with relief. "Just promise me that you will be careful, though, anyway. I love you, Mom."

"I love you, too, baby. You do the same," she counseled, her mama spidey-senses tingling as an automatic reflex.

With everyone seated around the table, it felt great to

be all together again as a family. Even the men appeared to put their questionable dislike for each other aside for an evening of pleasant conversation.

Meg and Kieran were only on the phone for an hour before they had to go to bed (it was way into the wee late hours for them) but they filled us in on how well his mum recuperated from her rib fracture and how they were settling into domestic, yet temporary, bliss.

Kieran finally finished recording his Celtic rock band's first album, and in just two more months, it was set to be released to the public. Gov's, his father's bequeathed pub, has now been sold to his business partners and he was free to live life as a romantic nomad. It suited him, that kind of existence.

Meg, completely enamored with her new life, was contemplating leaving the advertising world altogether—something I never expected her to do in all the adult years I've known her. Instead, she wanted to pursue her lifelong dreams of traveling and writing, and planned to continue her exploration of the world well after our trip to Spain.

Mia shared about her last two days in Italy, surprising us with the fact that she did not see Francesco after that night, keeping to her intention of having alone time. She spent one of her days entirely in an off-alley bookstore, wrapped up in a novel and indulging in cappuccino and decadent pastries.

On her last day, she went back to the Bardini Garden, where she sat and reflected on her journey and how much her experience in Florence healed her heart. Nature soothed her soul and reminded her about the important things in life. She came home refreshed and ready to juggle double duty as a single mother and restaurant owner—something she planned to jump on after our trip to Spain. Since we offered to help, she already had an idea of how we could all pitch in, too.

Great, I thought sarcastically.

Mom received another lecture opportunity, this time in California, and announced how she and Bruce would be taking this first trip together as a couple to Los Angeles. She radiated with joy, and with the way he looked at her, I could tell it was mutual. It made my heart soften a bit for the guy. I guess I could lighten up where he was concerned—only until he gave me a reason not to. He wasn't completely off the hook yet.

Granny was ready for her own adventure. Inspired by our journey, she joined a senior citizen traveling group, which took day tours to different museums, historical landmarks and even casinos. This weekend's trip was at the Museum of Modern Art in the city; a place I have visited so much that I practically had the blueprint memorized. She was so excited to be having lunch inside the museum with a few old girlfriends of hers who would also be joining her on this trip.

"Maybe next time I go, Marissa, I will see one of your paintings on those walls," she mused with pride. Granny had so much faith in me—much more than I had in myself.

As I looked around at my loved ones sitting at the table, I realized that everyone was in such a great place in their lives—including me, now that I was free to love Josh in the open.

But of course, that fragile sense of peace can never last long in this family; an incoming call from Mia's ex-husband, Kevin Logan, quickly changed the mood from serene to anxious.

When she heard he had news to share about Jordan Kissinger, the maniac who has been terrorizing us since we started this adventure, she put the call on speaker so we could hear for ourselves straight from the cop's mouth.

"They got them, Mi. They caught the bastard—and his accomplice. Allegedly, the Marinos were behind it all along."

Shock filled the room. Could it be true? Could this nightmare finally be over? Kevin waited a beat before continuing so we could catch our breath.

"After we failed to find a Jordan Kissinger spelled traditionally, it wasn't that hard to find an alternate that fit the description of the perpetrator. Apparently, a J-O-R-D-E-N K-I-S-I-N-G-E-R has quite the rap sheet—and a connection that gives him a motive." Pause for effect.

"He's Peggy Marino's older brother."

"I knew it," I pointed out. "I knew this had to be connected to one of them."

"You were right," he continued. "Did some checking into this guy to see what he was capable of. Never had a violent record before, though. Petty theft, drug possession. But sometimes in these cases, it escalates to more. Maybe he saw dollar signs and a way out.

"But that's what the authorities will hopefully get out of him. He's in custody now. So far, he is pleading innocent, but the evidence is stacked up against him. He wasn't at work the last three weeks—claiming he needed to take a leave of absence for mental health reasons. We're still investigating his whereabouts in April.

"Found the phony passport matching the traditional spelling of the name used at the airport and a crumpled up boarding pass in his glove compartment. Guess from where to where? Oh, and along with some cocaine, of course."

"Wow. So, who was his accomplice?" Mia asked.

"Peggy herself. She is also in police care. It started out that we were just going to question Peggy and the rest of the Marino family as standard procedure.

"Turns out, one of the officers who questioned her noticed the brooch she was wearing matched the description of the one Mia planted. While he stalled her, the team got a warrant to search the house and lo and behold, they found the fake jewelry box in her room.

"She is claiming her brother mailed it to her as a gift last week, and that she didn't know it was connected to Leigh's maternal family heritage. Kisinger's protesting that he never left her the box; that he's never even seen it.

"They are quite the pair—turning on each other to save their own ass. Very common in these kinds of situations; always happy to sell the other out to get a better deal."

"Do the police think there is any chance they are telling the truth?" Bruce queried. I thought he didn't get involved in family matters?

"Not likely with all the evidence, but we're keeping the investigation open. We can't rule out a setup—we never know if someone outside of the family is trying to make it look like it was an open and shut internal job. We have to consider all possibilities still at this point.

"However, a couple of the other family members—except her husband Patrick—confirmed Peggy's belligerence at the will reading and then weeks of her complaining afterward about not knowing anything about this inheritance, touting that her husband legitimately has a right to it.

"We've questioned Patrick, and although he seems to check out as not being involved in the scheme, we've advised him not to leave town. We're not letting anyone off the hook just yet," he warned.

"Good," I spat. "I want them to pay for doing this to our family. Whatever it takes to make them rot in jail, Kev, do it."

"You know I'll do what I can, Mar, but I can't get emotional about it. I have to follow the rules and thoroughly investigate this. That means I need my officers to speak with each one of you again—plus Kieran, Jay and your cousins. Everyone who knows anything."

"Of course," we all said in layered unison.

"One last thing," Kevin warned. "Keep your guards up. This isn't over. Even if it turns out Jorden and Peggy are guilty, we still don't know what lengths they have gone to already. For all we know, they could have a contingency plan in case they got caught."

"Like enlisting Dominic Moretti again," Mia pointed out.

"Well, the bug planted at Casa Bianchi is still in effect, so we are monitoring that as well to make sure that family doesn't get involved again. We're making sure to cover all angles," Kevin explained as he wrapped up the call. "Just stay safe, everyone, and call me if you have the slightest concern or uneasiness."

Thanking him for the information, we all promised we would be careful and keep him informed. One way or another, this mess was about to come to a conclusion soon.

3

Walking into my apartment after a dramatic family dinner and a short nightcap at Josh's, I found Jay passed out on the couch surrounded by crushed bags of chips, almost empty bowls of salsa and guac and bottles of beer all over.

As sweet as this guy was, he certainly was a pig. I knew he would eventually clean up after himself, but sometimes I would love for the house to stay tidy for just one day. Who needs kids when you have Jay?

My entry must have startled him awake, as he jumped and grabbed a beer bottle in defense at the sound of my keys clinking onto the counter.

"It's just me," I said, muffling a giggle.

"Ugh, Riss. You scared me," he grumbled sleepily.

"Why are you always so jumpy?"

"Gee, I don't know. Maybe because you are mixed up in some crazy family adventure with stalkers and potential murderers out there."

Okay, I know—I shouldn't have told him about my family secret. I already had this argument with Meg several times over. But it's Jay. I've known the boy since the third grade and I trust him with my life. Even if he was a big weirdo at times. Besides, he has a right to know if his life is in danger—what if the psychopath came to our front door?

At least with Jay here, I felt a little safer. His black belt ass could karate chop the life out of an intruder.

"Not anymore," I revealed. "Seems like they caught the jackass. And his sister—that Peggy Marino woman who wanted to protest the will."

He looked at me confused—I wasn't sure if it was because he was still coming out of a deep sleep or if he really wasn't catching on. He insisted that I take him through the whole story and by the end, he finally understood that we were no longer in danger.

"So, the jewelry box was a fake?"

"Yup. Mia had the brilliant idea to create a decoy to throw them off track. Oh, and she also added a real, expensive old lady brooch and a fake legacy note inside so the idiot would buy its authenticity, at least initially. Turned out better than we could have ever imagined, since it brought upon their downfall."

"Interesting," he responded, becoming more hushed and contemplative. I could tell that brilliant academic mind of his was turning its gears.

"Kevin told us, Josh and Bruce tonight that he'd have more questions for all of us. You, too, since you know about it. He just wants to make sure all angles are covered."

"Sure. No problem," he paused. "Wait—you mean Josh was there?"

"Yeah," I nervously confessed. "I finally told my family and brought him to dinner. They loved him."

And there it was. The disapproving look—Jay's own little green monster. We were twins in that way, equal in tempers and envy, though he covered it much better than I did (most of the time). He did have a kinder overall disposition—always a gentleman holding open the doors, chatting it up with the little old ladies at the grocery store and otherwise charming even the grumpiest of bosses. He reminded me of my dad in that sense.

Currently a traveling salesman by trade, he was a struggling artist like me, waiting for that big music break. He could sing the most poetic verses while skillfully running his fingers over the strings of a guitar, his eyes closed and lost in the moment. Like he could be in a crowd yet only need to play for his party of one; his soul.

He really had a gift, not unlike Kieran and his keyboard, but more alternative and acoustic in nature than my soon-to-be brother-in-law. I looked over and saw that vulnerable musician mixed with grumbled irritation.

I didn't understand where his jealousy was coming from, though. We were always friends; never crossed that line. He was like a brother to me. Guess that's what it was. He's just overprotective. Especially with everything that has gone down lately.

"Happy for you," he managed with a forced smile as he got up to walk towards his bedroom.

"Why don't you like him?"

"I like him just fine," he said defensively in his pseudo-Puerto Rican accent. "I'm just tired of listening to you guys have sex all the time while I'm not getting any. Thanks for giving me a break and going to his place tonight, by the way."

"I don't get it, Jay. Why *aren't* you getting any?" I questioned. "You are hot. Any girl would want to be with you."

That was the truth. With his Latin roots, his hair was as dark as mine with luscious curls that twirled around his striking face and heartbreaking sapphire eyes. He was a bit on the tall and awkward side, yet there was something about the way he carried himself that exuded pure sexiness. Must be that tropical blood of his.

Looking at him just now, it made me wonder why we were never more than friends…

"I don't want just any girl, Riss. You know that's never been my style."

"I know. You're too good a catch to pass on, though. Get yourself out there and find that woman!"

"My heart's not ready to move on just yet," he sighed heavily as he waved me good night and closed his door to indicate he was done talking about this.

When he first moved in with me after we realized we could help each other financially, he had mentioned being in love with a woman who just wanted to be his friend, and it was hard for him to just settle for someone else.

It amazed me that a man this good-looking was a one-woman type of guy, instead of living up to his womanizer potential. Meg loved to tease him, calling him a hopeless romantic.

He confessed he thought he needed to earn more money so that he would be "enough" for this woman. He joked how he would have to find some kind of pyramid scheme to get involved in, since he didn't think he'd be winning the lottery anytime soon—and especially since no surprise legacy was waiting for him with a rare green diamond ring or jewel-adorned mini treasure chest.

He would do anything just to give her the world, he said. Now there was a broken-hearted puppy dog if I ever saw one. If only he could reset himself with a one-night stand, he might be able to move on.

The next morning, I found him still brooding on the couch, his hair a wet mop after a fresh shower. I could tell something was bothering him, so I sat down beside him as he instantly blushed and turned away.

Oops! I quickly looked down to see a nipple had fallen out of my black nightie and tucked it back in with a nonchalant apology. Nothing he hasn't seen before.

"What's wrong?" I asked. Clearly irritated, he got up off the couch and made his way over to the kitchen for some more black coffee.

"Nothing. I think I need to take a ride to clear my head."

"Give me a minute to throw clothes on. I want to come," I pleaded. I had missed our motorcycle rides while I was in Italy. It was "our thing" ever since he got his first bike in our early twenties.

"Riss, not now," he tried to deter me. I know he needed to ride to get space, for whatever his broody reasons, but did he not know me and my persistence by now?

"Why not?" I looked up at him with the eyes I knew he couldn't resist. One way or another, I was going to cheer my second favorite fella up. Reluctantly, he leaned back against the counter and motioned for me to hurry up and get dressed before he changed his mind.

Sliding behind him onto the back of his Harley always gave me the goosebumps. The way his masculine body fit into his leather jacket and tight jeans—and how his hair tucked into a helmet with a few tendrils peeking out— was just like out of a cologne photo shoot.

I loved putting my arms around his waist and feeling him tense up at my touch. Even though we were just friends, there was something electric about it all (though not in a disrespectful way to Josh).

He smelled exceptionally good today, too. The fresh rain shampoo mixed with my jasmine body wash (guess he ran out of his) and some musky aftershave was an interesting combination to say the least, but for whatever reason, I was digging it. It kind of suited him—*tough, yet girly on the inside,* I snickered to myself. Totes appropriate.

He barely let me get on before he sped off onto the highway, cuing that even though I was there, he still wanted silence to think. I put my chin up against his shoulder and let the wind pass through both of us, tangling my hair into a delightfully knotted mess.

Exhilarating, liberating, adrenaline-pumping. Every single time I got on this bike with him I was transported to another world of danger and freedom. And he was pushing it to the limit this time, rushing carelessly around curves and jutting in and out of lanes. I loved every second of the thrill.

When we finally got back to the house, he quickly jumped off and went straight inside, still not speaking to me. I followed quietly in after him, removing my helmet and placing it onto the table next to his. I just couldn't let it go—against my better judgment.

"Jay, what the hell is going on with you? You've barely said a word to me all morning." He turned and looked at me in a way he never had before. Heated. Angry. Desperate.

"Let it be, Riss," he clearly warned with such raw emotion.

"No, I won't let it be. Why are you so worked up?"

"Having a shitty day. That's all," he insisted.

"No, that's not all. You've been moody since last night—ever since I told you about the Marinos being captured and Josh coming over for dinner. What's the deal?"

He stood there, his jowls throbbing in and out as he tried to soothe his own temper. I was not helping matters with all my pushing, but I thought he needed to talk and let it out. Sometimes we all need that prodding.

"Jay! Fucking talk to me already. I'm your best friend. Is this still about some stupid girl you can't seem to get over? She's not worth it."

That did it. I'm an insensitive shit who speaks before she thinks and is a master at hitting a nerve. But I didn't expect such a volatile reaction.

Without warning, my typically calm and gentle friend moved over to where I was standing near the front door, pinning me against the wall with his palms surrounding my head and his legs spread out blocking mine so that I couldn't move.

His body was so close to mine, not even a half inch away from touching, but even in his anger, I could tell he'd never harm a hair on my head. Yet still, there was contained rage brewing.

He just stared into my eyes with an intensity that scared me, intrigued me and aroused me all at once. His breath was a second away from my lips, his face right up against mine. I found it hard to swallow, waiting for him to spit out what I felt him longing to say.

"I said, let it go." He meant business. He refused to move from his stance, his eyes searching and pleading for me to either stop or figure it out myself. I could feel the burn from inside him as his body heat rose between us, and I admit, it was a little alarming.

"Release me," I whispered angrily. Shocked at his own actions, he apologetically freed me from his body cage and cursed himself as he moved away.

"I'm sorry, Riss. I didn't mean to lose my temper like

that," he said, looking over at me with genuine regret.

"I can't help you if you don't tell me what's wrong," I softened, sensing he didn't need my matching temper. I walked over to him and embraced him in a hug instead. He clung to me as if for dear life before gently pushing me away. At least he was much calmer now; even soft spoken.

"I can't do this anymore. I tried, but this isn't working. I—I have to go. I'm sorry."

"Go where? I don't understand. I want you to talk to me," I practically begged him to open up and let me in. "Please. I don't want you to go."

"I just think it's for the best that I move out," he said as I glared at him in disbelief. Where was all this coming from?

"Listen, Riss. I haven't been completely honest with you, and I haven't always done the right thing by you. I need to set things right," he rambled. "Besides, you have Mr. Moneybags to take care of you now, and I'm sure he doesn't need some male *best friend* hanging around," he pointed out sarcastically.

That stung, but he was right; him living with me was a source of ongoing contention between me and Josh. Yet still, I didn't want to lose this man from my life. Even if he did just insult me by inadvertently implying I was a gold digger…

"Jay—wait," I tried, but he just shook his head and walked away. I watched him, baffled, as he went to his room, threw a few things into a bag and walked towards the front door.

"I'll make sure you have my half of the rent until you find a new roommate, though I think we both know where that's headed. I'm going to crash at Dave's until I can figure things out. I'll grab the rest of my things once I land somewhere."

He looked back at me remorsefully, almost pausing as if not really wanting to leave. I couldn't find the words to stop him, but the confused tears that began falling spoke volumes.

"I never meant to hurt you, Marissa. Or anyone else. I hope you can forgive me." And with that, Jayson Rivera walked out of my door and possibly out of my life, without notice or explanation.

I didn't think I would feel this saddened over his departure. The apartment felt empty—not like when he went away on a weekend business trip. I always knew he was coming back. But he wasn't this time, and I still had no idea what the hell he had gotten himself mixed up in or what made him want to leave me; leave *us*.

He was my best friend—next to Josh, of course. I hadn't realized how much I missed him in my life until he sauntered back in earlier this year with a proposition I couldn't refuse. I had just lost Tony as a roommate because I made the mistake of sleeping with him and needed a replacement, stat.

I knew I couldn't repeat that mistake for a fifth time (yeah, habitual issue—and yes, one of them was a woman, so it's not like it matters whether I get a male or female roomie). I made that clear to Jay when he signed up to be my new co-tenant and begged him as my oldest friend not to let me screw this up; to stay strong if I got weak.

But luckily, Josh entered my life around the same time, so even if I were tempted to fail yet again, I was rescued by my new lawyer lover. It seemed to have worked, and despite his messy habits, Jay and I really got along well. I had no idea that something "wasn't working."

He just completely blindsided me. It made me wonder if I really was the problem after all—and if it wasn't just about my sexual habits like I had thought. What if I was simply intolerable as a roommate?

The thought scared the hell out of me, considering I was in love with Josh and had already started dreaming of us moving in together one day. I had even thought for a brief moment that this could be a sign for us to take the next step now that Jay moved out.

Apparently, Josh did, too. When I told him what went down, he immediately suggested that I move in with him and let Jay keep the apartment to himself. The idea terrified me, and I told him as much.

"I'm not sure I'm easy to live with," I admitted.

"You think I haven't figured that out already on my own?" he teased. "I know exactly what I'd be getting myself into. And I'd love every minute of it. Waking up to those beautiful eyes every morning, kissing those lips every night. It will make the rest of the day bearable," he joked.

"Cute, real cute," I laughed. "I'm serious though. I'm like a magnet for living arrangement destruction. What if you fall out of love with me?"

"That could never happen, Mar. I know you've had bad luck with roommates—but that is all they were. I love you and am willing to go the distance to be with you. I want to spend the rest of my life with you."

He leaned in to kiss me and instantly I felt reassured. I was still hesitant about making such a big move, though. I would be giving up the apartment I'd lived in for four years, and I'd be on his turf. Knowing him, he wouldn't let me pay a dime towards rent (ask me how often I've paid for anything on a date). So…

In addition to being with the man I loved, it could be exactly what I needed to bartend a little less and focus on my art a little more. No, I wasn't really a gold digger. But if my love wanted to support my dreams, how could I refuse his generosity?

"Okay," I said cautiously. "Let's do it."

I began packing up my things immediately and planned to move in by the end of the weekend. Jay was not happy when I told him, but he really had no say in the matter, especially since he was the one who left me. He did, however, agree to move back into the apartment and re-lease it in his name, only until he found another roommate.

Things between us were tense for a while, though after almost thirty years of friendship, we didn't want things to end on a sour note. He even sent flowers and a housewarming gift to congratulate us. It was a start, at least. Although he refused to confide in me about what was going on with him, he still wanted a place in my life and said he would always be there for me. I believed him. I needed to believe him.

Everything fell into place after the move. It all happens for a reason, they say. Josh had an extra office that I was able to use as an art studio, and I went to work on my Florence-inspired paintings and sculptures. Oh, how I loved bringing my visions to life.

I was able to cut back on my hours at the restaurant so I could focus on my creative work, thanks to Josh's financial support. Besides, since we lived in uptown Manhattan, the commute was now much longer and sucking precious time out of my day. Josh suggested that I quit altogether and wait until I returned from Spain before I found something else closer to home.

Home. I was in a home—*our* home. Family dinners continued each Sunday, and I was excited to be able to finally host one in a beautiful dining room when it was my turn. Since my apartment was too small, I had always arranged for us to dine out locally. Convenient, but never cozy.

Now, I was able to put out my own fancy dinnerware and try on a chef hat—after all, how much different from baking could cooking possibly be? A few recipes later and I was ready to be Martha Stewart.

Yes, I could get used to this kind of happy life, especially now that we no longer had our stalkers to worry about.

More evidence was found against Jorden and Peggy; enough to keep them locked up and away from us all. Police had found paper in Jorden's office desk that matched the type he used when leaving us threatening notes in both New York and Italy; the blurry image from the Dublin hotel matched his body build and hair color; he could not vouch for his whereabouts in April (an undocumented "business" trip); and the shipping package retrieved from the recycling bin at Peggy's house confirmed the jewelry box was sent from her brother.

Not a peep has been heard or a disturbance recorded anywhere since they were arrested. With Meg now back in the U.S., there have been no attempts to retrieve her ring, or to find the real box now that Mia's decoy was exposed as a fake.

No more threatening notes about those or about finding our final piece in Spain, and believe me, security has been monitoring us 24/7. We had every reason to believe we were in the clear.

The only sadness we experienced over the last month was hearing of our dear cousin Sorella Maria's passing. A grief-stricken Francesco said she went quietly in her sleep; in fact, that very evening she had claimed how her life was complete now that she was able to see her grandparent's home once again and fulfill her promise to our Nonno Leigh.

We held a candlelight procession in her honor at Granny's local church and grieved her over a traditional Italian dinner courtesy of Mia. We will never forget the blessing of meeting her and learning all about our Italian heritage.

But now, it was time for us to focus on our next, and final, adventure: Barcelona, Spain.

4

The Spain trip was going to work a little differently than the previous two. Our cousin connection there, Edward John Rubio, is actually an American citizen living in New Jersey, and we arranged to meet up with him this Saturday. He was going to fill us in on some of the backstory before joining us on our journey to his ancestor's country.

Edward John—EJ as he insisted we call him—was an eccentric little character. Named for his great-grandfather, Eduardo, he had been born and raised in America after his father, Matteo, moved here and married his sweetheart, Gloria. An only child whose mother passed when he was five from a fatal car accident, he proudly carried on the Rubio name.

Dedicated to his career, EJ didn't marry the love of his life, Rodney Anderson, until they were well into their fifties. He admitted that they thought they were too old to consider having surrogate or adopted children themselves, yet found joy in spoiling all of Rodney's nieces and nephews, of which there were many.

Though his grandfather's brother had married two different women and was thought to have illegitimate children all throughout Spain, none have been officially documented—until recently when those ever-popular DNA ancestry tests revealed a surprising family match.

However, as the current heir and a lover of the whole legacy idea and meaning behind the statue (yet to be revealed, he declared), EJ was more than happy to pass it on to his distant American cousins as requested. He agreed with Leigh's assessment that it should go to a fellow art connoisseur.

"Are you an artist as well?" I inquired.

"You could say that," he hinted, his cherub-like smile taking over his chubby European, pink-colored face with hazel eyes and balding brownish-gray hair. He's considered a young cousin in my grandfather's generation, though none of us could figure out what number or how many times removed he would technically be.

He had an inventive, unique style—wearing a casual short-sleeved, totem-printed, button-down shirt with weathered jeans and colorful oxfords. I should have guessed what his profession was.

"I'm actually the owner of the Rubio Art Gallery in Manhattan," he said with pride.

"Oh my gosh, how did I not make that connection before?" I gasped. "I love it there! The *Haunted Beings* sculpture exhibit is daring and marvelous!"

"Why, thank you. It's one of my favorites, as well," he replied. "I hear you are quite the *artiste* yourself." I blushed at the thought of someone actually calling me an artist.

"Not exactly. I've done a few paintings and sculptures in a home studio, but nothing on display."

"Since when are you so modest, Mar," Meg teased. "Her work is beautiful. I have no doubt she will have her own exhibits on display one day." I smiled at the thought of my big sister being proud of my creations. Maybe she has turned a new leaf and is paying more attention to my life, after all.

"I would love to see your pieces sometime. Perhaps when we get back from Spain, we can talk about bringing in some starters as a seasonal exhibit to gauge public response," he proposed.

"That—that would be amazing," I gushed. "Thank you."

"Very well, that's settled. Now, shall we talk about what's in store for you in Catalonia?"

He went on to explain that although considered part of Spain geographically, Barcelona technically belonged to an autonomous region known as Catalonia. In fact, many of its citizens spoke the dual languages of Spanish and Catalan—a dialectic blend of Spanish and French. Looks like my high school studies may not be enough, after all, though I think a few common phrases I've picked up from Jay's family throughout the years might help me with some lingo.

I thought I'd need to invest in another translator, but EJ assured us that we could get by with basic Spanish and even some English. Although he didn't live there, he was brought up speaking the language and would be there by our side to help us navigate the glorious city.

He mentioned how he had only been to Barcelona a handful of times throughout his life—more recently over the past year after Leigh approached him. Our grandfather had asked him to help bridge the gap between his Spanish heritage and the family's immigration to the United States, and EJ was more than willing to oblige.

He understood how Leigh wanted to keep the legacy alive, and that it would be best if the journey took us abroad to experience it firsthand. EJ himself was enthralled with the mystery, and painstakingly took on his self-appointed role as "Heir Master," he proclaimed.

"Leigh didn't miss a thing," he revealed. "He even knew about our DNA discovery and located my lost cousin, Teresa Balles. Although Leigh didn't tell her about the legacy per se, he did form a relationship with her so that she would be willing to sublet her Barcelona house to her American kin—like a timeshare. Such a convincing little devil," he chuckled.

Once EJ heard of Leigh's passing and our projected timeline for arrival, he enacted the plan to provide Teresa with an all-expense paid, two-week trip to her dream destination of Australia in return for the Airbnb-type trade. She was more than happy to accept the generous offer, and invited EJ and his husband to stay with her a few months ago when he traveled there to set our adventure in motion.

He said she was a delightful, mousy bookworm of a woman who was surprisingly thrilled at the thought of spending time in the Outback. Her home was impeccably tidy, everything in its place—and as long as we promised to keep it that way, she had no problem with the arrangement. She did hope to meet us one day as well, she said.

Perhaps she would end her trip a day early and join us for the planned family celebration.

Oh yes, part of the plan was to bring all of us together in the end—us sisters, Mom, Granny, our loved ones, our country-hosting cousins—everyone was invited to the grand reveal party in Barcelona on day thirteen.

Though I think for Teresa, he made arrangements for a family brunch on our final day instead to preserve the secrecy of our trip. Either way, it would be nice to meet the woman who generously put us up in her home.

"Will Rodney be joining us as well?" Mia asked.

"Oh no, cuz. He's offered to hold down the fort while

I go on this little adventure. He's a bit jealous, of course, but super supportive. I promised him a place at the party table, and we'll spend a second honeymoon there after that's over, so he's tickled pink over that idea. Just you and me, ladies!"

"So, how will this all work?" Meg asked, always the planner.

"Well, I'll be flying out with you and getting y'all settled into the house. We'll do some touristy stuff and then I have to take care of some business—you know, statue stuff," he winked at Marissa, "and then we'll get right down to it. No use in playing cat and mouse too long, especially with all the trouble that seems to be following you."

"Actually, that's been resolved," Meg informed him. "They have charged our grandfather's paternal relatives with all related crimes as of right now, and there have been no further threats or trouble."

"However," Mia interrupted, "we'll still have bodyguards and want to make sure the local authorities are monitoring the house we are staying in. I'd rather be safe and vigilant," she asserted.

"Smart cookie. I agree—I don't need the beets kicked out of me protecting some statue, as gorgeous as he is."

"He?" I poked.

"Ha, never you mind, cuz. All in due time," he warned playfully. "Point is, I agree with Mia and would rather be careful. You never know who could be lurking around in the shadows."

We all consented, then parted ways. With only a few days left to go before our final trip, the girls and I had some initial planning to do and lots of packing left. I was becoming more excited by the day. I was finally going to embark on my mission.

I couldn't decide what dresses to bring, or what to leave behind. The weather was sure to be balmy, with its Mediterranean breezes and sweltering end-of-summer sun. As I was trying to decide between a basic black tank dress and a silky red floral one, I felt his warm arms come up from behind me and smiled.

"I wish you were coming with me this time," I pouted.

"We've been through this before. You need this time with your sisters, and I have a case that I need to wrap up. I'll be there for the party. I promise," he cooed as he kissed the side of my neck.

"It's just not fair. Meg got to be with Kieran, and Mia with Francesco. Why must I go lover-less? Why must you torture me so?"

"It will be torture for me as well, babe. But I'd just want to keep you locked up in a room and you'd never see the sights of Spain or do your legacy thing. Besides, I hear absence makes the sex grow stronger," he implied, bringing his hands from behind his back to stroke my taut breasts.

He pulled me into a luxurious kiss, the dresses falling free of my hands so I could draw him in against my body to feel his full heat. His hands skillfully unbuttoned the front of my blouse, which carelessly fell to the ground in a slump—soon followed by my skirt, stockings and lace slip.

I purred as his hands wandered to my already hot and wet insides, pulsing me in preparation for what was to come. He tossed my suitcase and belongings from the bed so that he could lay me belly down and ass up, asking me to continue fingering myself while he watched and stripped off his own clothes.

He removed my hand from its frenzied state and licked each one of my fingers as he effortlessly glided into place. I could feel his fullness inside me as one hand reached around my left nipple to squeeze it and his other grabbed my ponytail.

Oh, this was not going to be slow and gentle, I noticed as he forcefully pounded me into rapid ecstasy before collapsing on top of me. He got up quickly though, throwing on his pants and shirt. I hated that he had to go back into the office instead of going another round.

"Oh, by the way, I just found this in the mailbox," he said as he grabbed a small, sealed blue envelope off of the dresser. "I was tempted to open it since it had your name on it…" he broke off, waving the note above my head humorously so that I couldn't reach it.

I think he just enjoyed seeing my naked body jiggle trying to get it. He finally relented, and what I read sent shivers down my spine.

"What is it, babe? I hope it's not from some secret lover you've been seeing on the side," he teased.

"Nothing. Just a thank you note from EJ," I covered. Thankfully, he was in such a rush to get to work that he believed me, giving me a kiss on the forehead on his way out the door, claiming he'd be home in time for dinner.

After he left, I took a good, long hard look at the note again.

Watch your back. I'm not done with you bitches yet.

I froze, not knowing what to do. I thought the Marinos were in custody. I thought this was over. Who could have sent this? Do I tell my sisters? Do I call Kevin and the cops? Why didn't I just tell Josh?

Questions were spinning through my head. I didn't want anyone to worry. I knew I should keep everyone informed, but what if they decided that it was not safe to go on this trip? Fuck, no. No one was going to keep me from this. No one.

We were going to still have guards, so we'd be safe. *Yes, we would be fine,* I convinced myself.

I wasn't going to fall into the same trap of fear everyone else gave in to. I was just going to tuck this into the tiny zipper of my luggage, just in case, and pretend it never happened.

As far as I was concerned, I'd watch my own back. If anything else happened, then I'd bring everyone into the loop. But not until I set foot on Spanish soil. I was going to get my statue come hell or high water.

At our last Sunday dinner before the flight, I was on edge. I'd like to think I had a good poker face, but I was beginning to doubt that. Josh had been questioning my uneasiness all week, but I chalked it up to just being nervous about what awaited me in Barcelona. No one questioned it was nerves.

I tried to let myself get caught up in the small talk and discussions over the landmarks we planned to visit while we were there. Even EJ and Rodney joined our family dinner, bringing quite the colorful conversations to the table. We all instantly adored them and their playful banter with each other. You could tell that they were meant to be.

As the evening drew to a close, I found myself alone in Meg's kitchen putting dishes in the sink when Bruce walked in. He had been quiet all evening, saying very little and faking a smile or polite response from time to time to seem engaged. I would say he was more of a people watcher than a contributor this evening.

"Are you all set for the big trip?" he asked, finally trying to make small talk.

"Yup. Packed and ready," I replied shortly.

"Marissa, I don't pretend that there isn't a distance between us. I'm hoping when you return, we can get to know each other a little better. For your mother's sake," he added.

"Sure," I responded, not taking my eyes off from rinsing the dishes. He stepped up beside me and turned the faucet off, waiting until I faced him.

"Do me a favor, please."

"A favor?" I barely knew this guy and he had the nerve to ask me for a favor?

"Yes. I know it seems like you are out of danger. But please, promise me you'll watch your back. Your mother couldn't take it if anything happened to you girls."

I cringed at the words—and at his grin that accompanied them. All color drained from my face, but I quickly turned back to the sink as if what he said wasn't a big deal. *Could it be?*

"Of course, I will. I'd never let anyone hurt me or my sisters," I informed him matter-of-factly with a cold stare down. Getting the hint that the subject was closed, he sighed and slowly exited the room.

Was that a veiled threat? Did he leave that note? Was Bruce somehow connected to all of this? He did appear to come into the picture and Mom's life at an all-too-convenient time: when Grandfather Leigh died. I wondered how much he really knew about our legacy.

But should I tell someone about Bruce—or the note? was the bigger question. I should probably alert the family cop, but Kevin might turn around and warn my sisters, and then Spain would be shelved for sure. *What should I do?*

"Ready to go, love?" came the familiar, welcomed voice from the doorway, breaking my distressed mind chatter.

I took a deep breath and decided it was best to just shake it off and forget what Bruce said. I was going to Spain. They would stop me if I mentioned anything, I'm sure. And would Mom even believe me if I told her Bruce was a threat? I know Josh would, but I couldn't start a family argument right then and there. Maybe I'd alert my ex-brother-in-law once I landed so he could take the necessary steps through the police force.

But first, I was getting on that plane and getting my damn statue.

"I am," I replied, turning around so he could see my bogus smile. "But I need to make a stop at my old apartment first. I left something there I need for the trip."

"No, you didn't," he protested. When I tried to negate him, he just held up his hand to stop me.

"Mar, it's okay. I know you just want to see Jay before you go. It's cool with me," he assured me, and I immediately felt better. In fact, he had a better plan than my fly-by goodbye.

"Why don't I do this? I'll drop you off so you can spend some time there, and you can just take a taxi back," he suggested, handing me a fifty-dollar bill.

I loved how he knew me so well. I did want to see my old friend and make peace with him before I left. Even though we texted now and again, I could use a cup of coffee and a chat with my sort of-maybe-still a bestie. It made me love Josh even more that he encouraged my visit, knowing how my two men were at odds with each other. Maybe even after all of this, they could learn to tolerate each other for my sake. At least, this temporary waiver of jealousy was a step in the right direction for Josh.

The door opened to a very surprised Jay wearing nothing but an old pair of gray shorts, the beads of perspiration covering his tightened chest and dripping from his hair. Obviously, I had interrupted an in-home workout.

"I'm sorry. I should have called," I said as I turned around to leave.

"No, Riss, it's fine. Come on in. I was just finishing up anyway." He opened the door fully and motioned for me to enter with a geeky, awkward smirk. "Sit down and make yourself comfortable. Mind if I grab a quick shower though? Do you have time for a visit?"

"That's why I'm here," I smiled at him. I could tell he was just as anxious as I was to have our first real conversation since our separation.

"Is Dave here?" I asked. His friend had agreed to move out of his studio apartment to move in with Jay, instead of the other way around. From what I've heard, things were working out really well that way.

"Nope. He's working. Hang on, I'll be right back. Grab a beer if you want," he offered while he scurried to the bathroom.

Not even five minutes later, he was out and more fully dressed in jeans and a black tank. *Wait—was he still using my jasmine body wash that I left behind as a stinging reminder I used to live here?* I chuckled to myself as he sat down on the couch beside me—though not too close. He was clearly keeping his distance.

"So, what brings you here?" he asked to break the ice.

"I'm leaving for Spain tomorrow. I thought it would be nice to catch up before I went."

"I'm glad you stopped by," he admitted with that beautiful smile of his. "I've missed you, Riss."

"I've missed you, too. Can we start over?"

"No need for us to start over. Let's just simply start a new chapter," he replied, always with a hint of poeticism in his outlook. True markings of a musician.

We chatted for a while; he filled me in on his latest escapades with Dave and the boys, and I shared what my sisters and I planned for Spain. He got a kick out of my description of my newest flamboyant cousins and wished he could have been there to meet them.

Although he still avoided confessing what he was truly up to, he mentioned that he had been cleaning up his mess and apologized again for leaving me high and dry.

We agreed to put it behind us and look towards the future. He even sat there as non-judgmentally as possible while I updated him on my relationship with Josh; he sweetly continued to wish me nothing but happiness, even though it pained him to do so. It gave me some hope.

It was like old times again, comfortably falling right back into place with each other. So much so, I felt like I needed to confide in him. He was the one person I could unburden my soul to; I knew he would have my back and do pretty much whatever I asked to make up for him abandoning me.

"Hey, can you do me a favor?"

"Name it."

"Can you keep an eye on my mom for me—well, more like on Bruce?"

"Of course. Why's that?"

I wasn't sure I should say anything further, but I knew I needed to get it all off my chest. If one person knew what was going on at least, I could rest easy knowing my family here was being watched over.

So, I told him about the note, and what Bruce said. Jay swore to keep it a secret, though he tried to convince me to alert the police and tell my family, practically pleading with me not to leave. But he knew me better than that.

And I knew him better—he was not going to let me go without promising that I would check in with him every single day and keep him informed of everything that was going on. Every last detail, he demanded.

"Or else," he warned with a serious look. "Don't make me get on a plane to Spain and track you down."

I had no choice but to concede and place my trust in him. I would do as he asked, and I knew he would keep me and my loved ones safe. *Please don't let me down,* I thought as I hugged him goodbye.

5

Holy shit, I'm in Spain, I thought to myself excitedly as we exited the gate and made our way to baggage claim. *We made it!*

I was bursting at the seams, unable to contain my glee. My sisters were equally joyful as we waited for EJ to get our rental car and drive us to our distant cousin Teresa's house.

"Can you believe we are finally here?" I squealed.

"This is it, Mar," Mia responded with fervor. "It's time for you to claim your heirloom and finish this for us!"

"I for one can't wait for this to be over, though," Meg added, evidently tired from the trip already. She was lagging behind and not her usual energetic self.

"Not that I'm not excited for you, sis," she quickly added, seeing my bubble burst a little. "I don't mean that at all. I just mean for this to be all over and we can settle back down into a normal life again."

I knew what she meant. Still, it was frustrating that she was ready to give up before we even started. Why couldn't she have the same enthusiasm for me that she had for Mia? But, I couldn't let her bring me down. I've waited too long for this.

The drive over to the house was your typical busy city commute. Traffic, honking cars—yet here, the profanities were either in Spanish or Catalan. I still wasn't trained enough to know the difference. Thank goodness EJ was already a master at navigating us through the foreign city.

Even though we were told we'd be staying in Teresa's house, I assumed that meant an apartment in a Barcelona complex. Boy, was I wrong, as we pulled up to a 5-bedroom luxury Spanish villa not far from the beach, in the southwestern neighboring coastal town of Sitges.

Located only about a half hour from the city center, the artsy town was famous for its beaches, renowned Carnival celebrations, historical museums and motor racing—all of which intrigued me. It's as if the village was designed just for me.

Teresa's home was simply gorgeous, with its pristine white, modern 4-floor structure, multiple viewing windows and palm trees bursting out in greeting. Walking up the terra-colored stairway, the front porch was enclosed in crystal clear glass panels to protect us from falling while gazing upon the Mediterranean Sea drawn out in front of us.

I found myself lost in the blue and white crystals as the sun beamed its light down to play. I closed my eyes to inhale the salted scent of the sea and imagined the warmth of the water engulfing my body in bliss. I couldn't wait to dance within the waves that called to me.

Continuing on our tour, the inside of the villa was just as incredible as its exterior. Contemporary Ibizan style all the way—its whitewashed walls, polished floors and colorful paintings accenting the purity. Aside from the front door and lobby area, the first floor seemed to only house a master bedroom suite and bathroom.

I walked into the dream knowing this would be my personal space, separated from everyone else. A large king-sized canopy bed welcomed me into its soft white embrace, colored only by a couple of red throws and pillows.

It seemed undisturbed and unused. Did Teresa even sleep in this room? Sigh, if only Josh could be here to indulge in the privacy of it all. I guess it was for the best considering this was a stranger's home after all, and we shouldn't disgrace her bed. But oh, the things I imagined we could do in here…

Moving on to the next floor, we found the living room with its spacious, comfortable yellow leather sofas (finally, some color in this place!), a family-style dining area and a kitchen that left Mia gasping as if she was having an orgasm on the spot.

Yeah, we would be dining on her interpretation of Mediterranean cuisine this week, that would be for certain. I saw the wheels of creation turning and the desire to shop rush through her very soul.

Off to the left, there was a smaller master bedroom with its own half bath, a room we agreed would be best suited for EJ as our not-so-humble host. He made even the most boring of house tours entertaining.

As forewarned, everything had its place. It almost made me afraid to walk around for fear of breaking one of Teresa's blown glass figurines on display. Small ballerinas and flowers, colorful animals and a large, intricate crystal village most certainly must have been imported. A quick check at a small green and yellow snake confirmed at least one of these was from Venice.

The third floor housed the remaining three bedrooms, which although not masters, were still luxuriously big with an adjoining bath. Obviously meant for Mia and Meg, they happily placed their suitcases on their respective beds and shrieked over their panoramic balcony views of the coast.

I noticed the third bedroom door was closed, however. Sneaking a smirk, EJ took my arm and guided me towards the room, gesturing for me to open it. Standing in front of me was an open room with only a desk in the corner, hidden by a huge easel, basket of paints and sculpting tools. I was speechless.

"Do you like it?" he asked. "Teresa barely uses this room, so when I approached her about setting it up as an art studio for you, she was delighted to oblige—as long as you leave behind a piece of brilliant artwork for her home, she requested."

"Oh, it's fantastic, thank you! Thank you so much!" I was so overwhelmed with emotion that I ran over to give him a great big bear hug.

"I already have an idea to paint a mural of blown glass images for her!" Pinch me! A studio just for me? This place was a *dream*. How was I ever going to leave here? Oh—by being dragged by the arm to keep moving, that's how, as I was quickly reminded by Meg.

We weren't done with the tour just yet, apparently, leaving the fourth floor as the *pièce de résistance:* a rooftop pool with a 360-degree vista of the city. Surrounding it was a huge lounge area filled with red striped cushioned chairs and white umbrellas—enough for a party of at least thirty. Noticing the barbecues and bar over in the right-hand corner, I was guessing that this would be where we'd have our final family party.

EJ suggested that he take his leave to freshen up and that we all do the same, leaving me to jump right into painting, Mia to probably read and well, Meg to do her planning.

We had a few hours before dinner, and I decided that I'd rather dine as an unkempt mess from traveling than give up the opportunity to feel those brushes in between my fingers.

Gazing at the perfectly primed white canvas in front of me, I let the paint colors take me away. Since I already knew what I wanted to make for Teresa, I started there, knowing that once I saw the city, I'd be distracted to capture a different visual.

I think that's why I haven't really been featured as an artist yet—I was never focused long enough to finish something. Truthfully, my Ireland series was the first I had ever completed in one sitting. Even Italy was still waiting for my final touches.

Before I knew it, Mia was gently knocking on the door to give me a 30-minute warning in case I did want to shower and change before we left. Grateful for her interruption, I decided that I was satisfied with my progress and could use the break.

Instead of driving, EJ guided us towards the super convenient public transportation that took us into the heart of Barcelona. There, the bustling of the nighttime filled my senses with exotic excitement, urging me to join in its dance of life.

He took us down to the famous Las Ramblas (or was it La Rambla? No one could give us a straight answer), a pedestrian promenade lined with trees, shops and restaurants of all kinds. The pavement swirled like waves with bright, colorful mosaics—from what we could tell in between the breaks of the crowds' feet.

I recognized one style of mosaic and EJ confirmed it was, in fact, a genuine Joan Miró. Holy crap. I was standing *on* greatness.

This place certainly was a hopping nightspot. Thankfully, EJ had already done his homework on prior trips and sourced out the best places to go. He first took us to a hidden gem—a cava bar—where he insisted that we needed to pre-game to kick-start our trip.

With no room to sit, we each ordered a glass of the champagne-like bubbly spirit and stood shoulder to shoulder. The sparkling wine was so refreshing, we insisted on buying several bottles to keep at the house for future dinners.

Next, we strolled down the boulevard, stopping here and there at souvenir shops, though we decided it would be best to come back another time for that, as we were already lugging around bottles of cava. This most definitely was a unique, cultural area: the live musicians and performers I expected; what I did not expect were the human statues and an erotica museum.

Note to self: come back when I'm on my own to explore that one.

We finally ended up at our destination, a little outdoor tapas dive café. Pitchers of red and white sangria filled the center of our table, as did an assortment of Spanish appetizers, ranging from patatas bravas (potatoes in a spicy sauce) and chicken brochettes, to grilled calamari and a platter of Spanish ham and manchego cheese with toasted bread dipped in a tomato and olive oil mixture. Everything was so delish.

We were so engrossed in our food and sangria that we almost forgot why we had come.

"So, which story would you like to hear first, my dears? Our American migration, or how my prestigious family fell from grace?" he ribbed.

"Ooh, let's do the juicy scandal," Meg selected, obviously feeling her peach and white wine beverage go to her head.

"All right then, the scandal it is!" EJ concurred.

He clearly savored divulging every salacious detail of his family's historic drama. He began with how we were really connected—our thrice-great-grandmother, Elena (the one who received the ring from Banan I when she married into the O'Sullivan line, he noted), was sister to Eduardo Rubio, EJ's namesake and great-great-grandfather.

"We were descendants from the royal House of Bourbon, albeit quite a few lineages removed from the throne line. Think of it as daughters with second born sons having second born sons multiple times over. Still of noble, royal blood and prestige, yet nowhere near being heir apparent," he explained.

"Elena and Eduardo were children of a younger son in that generation's family, Horace Rubio. Now, Horace was an ambitious one, always trying to figure out how he could wedge himself in line for the throne somehow. Unmistakably, that was an impossibility, but that didn't stop the devil from trying.

"He schemed and plotted and planned downfalls, even murders and attempts to impregnate the queen-to-be," EJ dramatically and deliciously acted out for us.

"He eventually was caught and charged with treason, shaming his family's name and stripping away all of their fortune. At the end of it all, he was left with no family or heritage; nothing but an old dragon statue his mother gave him as a token of his now deceased legacy."

He mentioned that he'd go into the history of the dragon statue at another time—but I was ever so intrigued to finally know what the statue's likeness was.

A dragon! How cool!

EJ continued on with his fascinating story, as if he

were performing a Shakespearean play.

As a result of his treachery, Horace's family was forced into middle class living, something so unfathomable to the old man, that he took his own life. In doing so, he left behind his wife and two teenage children to suffer his consequences.

Young Eduardo successfully found employment as a fisherman, earning him back some of the respect that was lost through his father. He was a hard worker, determined to provide his mother and sister with a strong foundation. Since Horace died before being able to arrange for his almost-of-age daughter's betrothal, that task now fell to Eduardo.

While working on the docks one day, he met an astute businessman from Ireland by the name of James O'Sullivan (husband to Agatha and father to Banan I, Meg reminded us). James had taken a liking to young Eduardo, admiring his work ethic and kind spirit.

He spent the better half of a day with the young lad, and when he learned of his family's disgraced legacy and his dilemma over his sister, it was James who proposed to join Elena and his youngest, Banan, in marriage.

It was a sad day for the Rubio family, as Elena did not want to be torn from her family; especially not from her sickly mother. But it was the only solution to make sure she was well provided for. Eduardo knew he would be responsible for his own wife and family one day and could not care for his sister indefinitely. This seemed like the best option for all.

Since the fallen Rubios had very little dowry to give in exchange for Elena, James and Agatha had mercy upon the young couple and gave them enough to live out their lives without struggle. Even though her immediate family was no longer of royal status, Elena was still a noble enough woman herself, with all the mannerisms and upbringing that would be appropriate as young Banan's wife.

Although there were a few gossips and whisperers, the Irish townsfolk respected James enough to honor his decision for the union, never questioning his reasons. Eventually, the young couple moved away to start a new life and fell in love.

"And you know the rest of the story from Colleen, if I'm not mistaken?" he concluded.

"Yes, thank you! That was an amazing story! Sad, but poignant. What a wonderful brother Elena had," Meg mused.

"Indeed," EJ agreed. "There's more to that story, too, but for another time I'm afraid. I'm wiped. Shall we retreat back to that superb villa for the night?"

We all agreed, feeling the grogginess set in. On our way back, EJ reminded us that he needed a few days to set everything up before Marissa could actually retrieve the statue—he first needed to go through an identification and clearance process, and while that was in progress, he had an overseas art transaction to attend to.

He'd be giving us the next three days on our own, though he did mention that he'd probably still crash at the villa a night or two in between. He suggested that we take full advantage of his absence.

Settling into the cushy bed, I looked over at my phone to see the light go off. I smiled as I saw the incoming text from Jay. I glanced at the clock and realized it must be close to dinnertime in New York.

How was your first day?

Incredible. This house is ridiculous. First floor master suite to myself. Third floor art studio. Rooftop pool. I mean, come on!

Sounds chill. Everything still cool?

No notes or weirdos. All good here.

Good. You forgot to text me when you landed.

Are you my dad now?

No LOL. But I'll be like one if you make me come out there to check on you. You promised me, Riss.

K. I'll text every day. Promise.

U better. Get some sleep. Love ya kiddo.

Right back atcha doll xo

I smiled, putting down the phone. I loved how we were back to our normal selves again. I was also glad I finally confided in someone about the note and about Bruce's spine-chilling words. I knew Jay would have my back, and I always liked the feeling that someone was protecting me. Not in a creepy way, but in a caring way.

Speaking of, I realized I should probably text my boyfriend good night!

I wanted to leave Josh a little love note so he'd know he was the last person I thought of as I went to sleep. I figured he'd be busy with work, but he quickly responded to tell me how he missed me and how cold and lonely the bed was without me.

Our exchange turned into a wonderful delay, as he FaceTimed me from his bed with a provoking visual.

Completely naked with a hard-on, he coaxed me into joining him in a little nighttime phone play. Not the same as the real deal, but it was still a pleasurable way to fall into a deep slumber after watching each other masturbate and orgasm. God, I couldn't get enough of this man.

After a wonderfully sound sleep, I awoke in the later part of the morning to a quiet, darkened room. I almost forgot where I was, thinking I was in a dream surrounded by all the softness. It felt amazing to just sleep in without having to get up and go to work at a pain-in-the-ass snob restaurant.

Based on our experience from our past two trips and bouts of jet lag, my sisters and I already agreed that we would take this first full day to relax and adjust, rather than jump right in to sightseeing. After all, who could resist a day sitting poolside on a roof overlooking the Med coast?

Lounging on a float in the pool and drinking a cava mimosa instead of my normal black coffee, I felt the warmth of the sun penetrate through my skin. Mia had already been up for about four hours, taking a walk around the grounds and finding a little nook to get lost in her latest crime novel.

Meg had the same idea as me, lazily sleeping as long as she could before venturing out to join me at the pool.

"This place is ridiculously amazing," she said. "I thought I was sleeping on a cloud."

"I know, right? This new relative certainly knows how to live in style!"

"What are you drinking?"

"Oh, this? It's cava with orange juice. There's one with your name on it right over there on that table."

"That's my girl! You're the best," she smiled as she grabbed another floating lounge and joined me in the pool. By then, Mia had made her way up towards us, sensing that we were past the morning cranky stage and ready for her early bird perkiness.

"This was such a great idea to just spend the day here," she mused. "I hope you don't mind, but before EJ left, I had him run me to the store to pick up a few items so I could make brunch and dinner here tonight. Figured I'd whip up a Spanish tortilla in a little while, and then try my hand later at paella."

"Sounds perfect, Mi. But before you do that, why don't you just relax and join us?" Meg invited.

I saw her hesitation—I knew that she had come a long way in having more self-confidence since leaving Italy, but she still struggled with her body image slightly. Even being twenty pounds down since then, I could tell she hated the idea of bathing suits and pools when anyone else was around.

"Come on, Mi. The water is warm, the sun feels incredible and I'd love to just chill in the pool with my sisters," I encouraged.

"Well, when you put it that way," she relented, finally disrobing to reveal what must've been a new leopard print tankini set—a huge leap from her regular, dowdy one-piece cover-ups.

"You look amazing!" I exclaimed and whistled. "What a hottie." I loved making her blush every now and then. She just needed to own her inner seductress, though I sensed there was more to my sister than she let on in that department. I saw the sparks between her and Francesco in Italy, and there's no way they tangled in lame missionary lovemaking.

For a few moments, the three of us floated around in silence, sipping our drinks and letting the sun beat down to form glistening beads of sweat on our bodies.

"So," began Meg, "how are things going with Josh?"

Now it was my turn to blush. I wasn't used to having such conversations that left me giddy and childlike.

"Surprisingly perfect. I thought for sure I would have screwed things up by now. But, he's different. He accepts me for who I am, and I don't have to pretend to be someone else to earn his approval."

"That's wonderful, Mar. So, he is treating you right?" inquired Mia. She'd never stop being the wife of a cop, divorced or not. Too many years of training.

I simply laughed. "Yes, he is. He's been footing a lot of our expenses so I don't have to work as much in the restaurant, which lets me focus on my art. Not that I'm in it for the money, but it really is a nice change of pace to not have to penny pinch."

"Seems like things are getting serious," Meg deduced. "I was surprised at how quickly you moved in after Jay moved out."

There it was. I knew sooner or later the condescending monster would rear its head.

"How come it's okay for you to live in another country with someone you just met a few months ago, but it's not okay for *me* to move in with the man *I* love?"

"No need to get defensive, Mar. I'm not judging—I'm just making an observation. There's a difference," she explained in her obnoxiously uppity tone. "All I meant was that you have never lived with a guy on purpose, with the intention of being more than a roommate. You are usually skittish of commitment. I just want to make sure you are okay, little sis. That's all."

"Oh." I guess I do have a tendency to defensively jump to conclusions, especially around her. "I get it. It surprised me too, to tell you the truth. Jay left so suddenly that it made me wonder why I could never hold down a roommate. I mean, I never slept with Jay, so I don't know where things went wrong."

I caught Meg and Mia exchange a joking glance, like two high school girls who knew gossip that I didn't.

"What?"

"What?" Mia asked. "Girl, are you really that dense?"

"Dense about what?"

"Jay!" Meg replied.

"What about him?"

"Seriously, Marissa? The guy is obviously crazy about you," Mia suggested.

"Wait—Jay? No way. He's like my brother. He would never think of me that way."

"Oh, no?" Meg challenged. "Have you ever caught him blushing as you paraded around in one of those silk nighties of yours? Have you noticed how protective he is of you? How about how damn jealous he is of Josh, and pretty much every guy that ever entered your life since you were kids?"

"Yeah, but that's because we're best friends."

"Okay, you keep telling yourself that," Mia laughed and dropped the subject to shift to another uncomfortable one. Bless my sisters and their persistence.

"So, how does Josh feel about you having a guy for a best friend?"

"He's fine with it." They both glared at me with a "yeah right" kind of look. "All right, so he's not thrilled about it. But now that we live together, he doesn't feel so threatened. He even let me hang out with Jay for a little while before I came here."

"Let you?" Mia questioned, perplexed.

"Not like that. I didn't need his permission—I think you both know me better than that. I mean, he willingly suggested that I spend time with Jay because he knew how much it would mean to me. He was cool about it. He's a great guy."

"He seems to be," Meg agreed. "I'm really happy for you, Marissa."

"Me too," said Mia. "But if he ever hurts you, he will have to answer to me."

"I hope you've said the same thing to Mom," I let slip.

"What do you have against Bruce?" Meg asked quizzically.

"Well, I found out about his ex-wife's claim of abuse, and even though he was found innocent, it still unsettles me. And I see the way he and Josh are leery of each other. I don't like the way he looks at me, either. He's always been kind, I guess, but there is something peculiar about him that I can't put my finger on. So, my guard is up."

"That's understandable," reassured Mia. "After so many years, we are all protective of Mom and want to make sure she is okay." Sensing this could probably turn into an all-out battle and ruin our day, the family peacekeeper once again steered the conversation in a different direction.

"I say we cherish this time we have together. Jorden and Peggy have been charged, and we have had no indications of any further threats. No notes, no stalkers, no disturbances. I believe we are free to enjoy this trip without worry, so why don't we do that? I'm going to whip us up a delicious tortilla and then we can talk about where we want to go tomorrow," she stated cheerfully.

"Let me know if you need help! I'm going to go hop in the shower," Meg responded.

I just nodded, hiding my guilt-ridden face behind big sunglasses so that it wouldn't reveal my suspicion that our danger wasn't over. But Mia was right about one thing—it had been quiet since arriving here in Spain, and hopefully it would remain that way.

6

A new day dawning, I couldn't wait to go out and about to explore the charms of Barcelona. Today was going to be "museum day," a trip to paradise in my book. I knew my sisters were not the biggest fans of art exhibitions, but they were totally accommodating of my need to take in as much culture as I could.

We started out at Museu Picasso de Barcelona, where—you guessed it—the entire building was dedicated to the works of Pablo Picasso, spanning a 20-year career. Of course, I was enamored with the display of Cubist paintings he is famous for—oh my God, to see them live, in person, was indescribable. The imaginative and daring play of lines and colors, turning an ordinary portrait into a genius defiance of traditional technique. Awe-inspiring, to say the least.

Even more fascinating than his late works were the primordial sketches of his youthful beginnings as an artist. They were more conventional in style, and it was an experience to see the transformation of his people-inspired art. He captured their essence in *Man in a Beret;* portrayed the reality of living on the streets in *The Wait (Margot);* and then completely recreated human beings in a new light when he painted one of his dearest friends in *Portrait of Jaume Sabartés.*

But there was so much more to see. His ceramic

pieces were exquisitely unique. I was equally enthralled with the personal photos of him that were donated by his photographer so that we could catch a glimpse of the man behind the masterpieces during the final years of his life.

If it weren't for my sisters urging me along, I could have spent the entire week digesting all of this wonderfully rich history. *Why is it that I am the one always rushed? I should be able to call the shots a little more on my journey, shouldn't I?*

Well, I didn't want to leave, but we had two more museums to fit into the day, they reminded me, so I acquiesced to finishing up my first tour. On our walk over to grab the metro towards the Museu d'Art Contemporani de Barcelona, we briefly stopped at a little local bakery for a light snack of Spanish hot chocolate and traditional Catalan xuixo: a sugary-topped, deep-fried pastry filled with scrumptious custard cream. *Muy delicioso!*

Bellies full and happy, we made our way to MACBA, as it is known, to wander our way through the "short century," featuring works from the early 1900s to today. Abstracts, colonial interpretations, modernism and decades of political debate in art form lined the great halls. This was diversity at its best—allowing perspectives from all over the world to blend together in harmony for the public to appreciate and admire.

Perhaps that is what magnetized me so passionately to art. There was an unspoken acceptance of individuality, and it gave me somewhere to belong.

Satisfied with MACBA, I then tormented my sisters for another hour as I gawked through the Joan Miró Foundation, perhaps one of the most beautifully designed museums in all the world. With its clean and contemporary shapes and colors, the designer, a friend of Miró's by the name of Josep Lluís Sert, clearly captured his essence by combining art with architecture.

Throughout the exhibitions, I grew increasingly inspired by the man's diversity in styles, ranging from cubism and poetic women to his darker surrealist and political exposés.

Of course, I couldn't be completely selfish and make it all about me, even though I wanted to. So, along our tour of the city, we stopped by the famous Park Güell for Mia, which was fine with me, since the grounds were a colorful mosaic tribute to naturalist artist, Antoni Gaudí. I was relieved to see it was much more than just some pretty flowers to look at.

I especially loved his *El Drac* creation, a multi-colored dragon/salamander that welcomed us into the park. It made me think of how EJ said my statue-to-be was in the form of a dragon, wondering what the significance of this mythical creature was in Spanish culture. I felt oddly connected to it. Like the dragon was my true spirit animal.

We strolled through the perfectly manicured gardens, Mia especially relishing in its biodiversity, from olive, oak and almond trees, to the aromatic native flowers and bushes of rosemary, lavender and magnolia. The colors danced within its vivid greenery, and the scents tickled our noses with soothing essences.

We stopped for a while to take in the serenity of our surroundings, hardly believing this peaceful gem resided in the heart of a busy metropolis.

Meg seemed to be more tired than normal on this trip, having to sit out a few exhibitions during the day and opt for metro rides instead of walking. She thought the jet lag was really getting to her since she'd been flying back and forth to Europe so often, but promised that she'd find the energy to keep exploring.

At her request, we visited the absolutely breathtaking and iconic Basílica de La Sagrada Família before the long afternoon drew to a close. The Basílica itself, still in progress, was a continued reflection of the work of Gaudí, magnificent to behold. We were able to enter one of the towers, from which we held our breaths to look out over the impressive view of Barcelona.

There also happened to be a special performance there of the acclaimed drama, *Misteri de la Selva,* written in an ancient romance language but easily understood through the beautifully expressed players. I have to admit, it was quite moving and touching.

Romance isn't really that bad, I mused to myself, thinking of my dear Joshua and how very much in love I was with the man. I can see why Meg was such a sucker for a great love affair.

Wrapping up the evening at a little nearby café, we indulged in more sangria and tried new tapas. We quite enjoyed these smaller dinner samplings in contrast to the fancy, multi-course banquets we indulged in while in Florence or the hearty meals in Ireland. Yet all of these trips have been incredible experiences I will never forget.

Tucking myself in for the evening, I looked forward to checking in with my love.

"And how was my girl's museum adventure today?"

"Oh my God, you would not believe everything I saw! Picasso, Miró, Gaudí—and so many contemporary artists. The colors, the textures, the symbolism and emotional portrayal; I couldn't get enough of it. Like I was whisked away into my own kind of fairy tale—a darker one, mind you, but another world altogether where I just felt, I don't know, at home. Understood. It really was a dream come true today."

"Good for you, baby. I am glad you are enjoying every moment." I heard something off in his voice as he said it. In fact, his whole tone was foreboding ever since he picked up the phone.

"What's wrong?"

"Don't worry about it, love. I want you to just focus on yourself right now."

"Cut the crap, Josh and spill it," I demanded.

"Okay," he acquiesced slowly. "Have you talked to Jay lately?" With a sense of remorse, I swallowed hard before answering.

"Yes. He made me promise to check in with him daily. I hope you're not mad."

"No, of course not. At least, not at you," he reassured me. "Not sure why he would make you promise something like that when I'm your boyfriend and he's not."

Ah, the resentful jab. That was familiar at least. I didn't bother to address it. I wasn't up for a male ego boxing round tonight.

"Say, have Bruce and Jay ever met?" he continued when I refused to acknowledge his petty comment.

"Hmm, not to my knowledge. I mean, they know of each other, but I don't think we've ever formally introduced them. Why do you ask?"

"I—I saw them together at the coffee shop on that corner by your old apartment earlier today. I didn't get close enough to hear what they were saying because I didn't want them to know I was there. They were rather intense. It just seemed so odd. I thought maybe you would know why they'd be meeting."

"That is pretty unusual. I'll have to ask him."

"Don't, Marissa. I'd rather you not talk to him at all,

actually. I don't trust him."

"Josh, I have known him my entire life. If he was meeting with Bruce, I am sure there was a damn good reason. Maybe he was just keeping an eye on him like I had asked."

"You asked—never mind," he stopped himself from scolding me, knowing with my growing terseness that he had to tread lightly. "Okay, but you didn't see them, Mar. They were mighty cozy for two grown men who had never met before. They are up to something. I can feel it."

"I think you might be overreacting."

"Seriously, I want you to stop talking to Jay for the moment until I can figure it out." So much for treading lightly.

"I'm sorry, did you just forbid me to speak with my best friend of over thirty years? What are you, a caveman?"

"No, but I am your boyfriend and you should respect my wishes," came the irritable response before he adjusted his tone to pleading. "Trust me on this. Please."

"This isn't about trust, Josh. This is about you controlling my life, and I won't be told what to do. If I want to talk to Jay and text him every day, I will. And don't you dare demand otherwise."

"Why is he so important to you? Are you in love with him or something?"

"What the fuck is wrong with you? I just finished saying I've known the man since we were children—practically my whole life. He's like a brother. Nothing ever happened between us and nothing ever will. Why can't you get that through your thick skull?"

"Because I see the way he looks at you. You are so oblivious, Marissa. He's trying to come in between us. And I know Bruce isn't my biggest fan, as I'm sure your mom told him I tipped you off about his divorce. So, maybe they are plotting against me."

"For goodness' sake, you are being paranoid and stupid right now. Josh, I love you. Nothing Jay or Bruce or anyone else says is going to change that. Except maybe *you,* if you keep this shit up."

"So, now I can't be concerned over your guy best friend, who you used to live with and practically walk around naked in front of? Who made you promise to keep in touch daily and then goes and suspiciously meets with your mom's boyfriend? I'm just asking for you to be cautious instead of impulsive."

"You can be concerned all you want. But I'm a big girl and can make my own decisions. And I'm not going to stop talking to Jay because your ego is bruised."

"You're impossible. How am I supposed to protect you if you are going to be so belligerent about everything?"

"Sweetheart, you haven't even seen belligerent. Tell you what. I'm going to go to bed, and you can take the rest of the evening to contemplate why being a Neanderthal is not the way to keep my heart. Good night, Joshua," I spat out, not giving him the chance to respond before hanging up the phone.

My fire was fueled—and not just over Josh. What the fuck was Jay doing with Bruce? True, he could've been doing just as I asked, but why didn't he tell me he had planned to meet him and keep me in the loop? Since I still had yet to text him today, I thought I'd do some investigative work of my own.

Just checking in. All quiet here. Incredible museum tours. How was your day?

Can't wait to hear about it. Day was normal. Work, gym, eat.

That's it? Sounds like an uneventful day. Nothing exciting to report?

Nope. Same old. Gotta run though. BNO.

K. Have fun.

You too. Stay safe xo

Same old, huh? Now I was truly pissed. Why didn't he just tell me about his little rendezvous with Bruce? What was he hiding? Even if he was going out for a "boys night out," he could have said he had to run, but that he'd fill me in later.

Now I understand why Josh was so miffed. Why would Jay lie to me?

Jay's omission was a lie. Josh's demands were juvenile. I was dealing with two little children.

That was it—I had enough of this stupid boy battle between them and now they were going to face the consequences. I wasn't going to contact either of them for a few days. See how they'd like that. No one tries to control or fuck around with Marissa Rossi.

The next morning, Meg was feeling a little bit under the weather, so we delayed our trip to the beach for a few hours so she could get some more rest. Still angry at the men in my life, I took the opportunity to close myself off in my little studio.

But I didn't want to finish painting my hostess gift or continue on with my Italian-inspired intentions. No, I wasn't feeling flowery at all.

It was darkness that consumed me. Anger, mistrust, betrayal, lunacy even. Not knowing who or what to believe, and quite possibly overreacting like I tend to do. It didn't matter. I picked up the dark colored palette and began drawing from deep within me.

The dragon popped into my mind. Not a cute little *Puff, the Magic Dragon.* A sinister, dark gray, scaly, green-eyed, pissed off beast breathing fire onto a red heart, turning it black. The sky was ominous with rain clouds and lightning in the background.

I painted for hours, frantically pouring out how I felt. How betrayed and annoyed I was by the two men in my life. How my tender heart inevitably was going to be consumed by the evil creature representing man.

Like the man who changed me for the rest of my life.

Oh no, I would never forget Mr. Terrance, my high school English teacher. The man I trusted, who promised he would help me pass the course so I could graduate— who wanted nothing more than to seduce the innocent child that I was.

It started all so innocuously. *Stop by after school and we'll go through the lesson,* he said. And so, I did. It just so happened to be a lesson in poets of the Romanticism Movement, where he'd first seductively read the words of Keats, Hugo and Lord Byron, and then engage me in deep conversation about their meaning.

He'd increasingly move in closer each time, and my teenage hormonal body became confused with the rush of lustful feelings and wetness building down below. *Was that normal?* I had the courage to ask him, as he made discussing sex such an easy topic to open up about. *Oh yes,* he would reply, and simply smile.

Paint, paint, paint. Darken the dragon scales and deepen the evil green eyes of the demon centerpiece.

It was Robert Burns' *A Red, Red Rose* that tipped the scale between conversation and physical touch. I could feel the love he "declared" for me as he demonstrated what that love did to his body as he cited the poet's words. I could see the hardened outline under his pants. I felt the curiosity as he encouraged me to touch…to open his pants and allow an exploration. He let me take a taste before he took my lips in a heated, twirling tongue kiss that sent electrical pulses through my young body.

He then took it upon himself to remove my skirt and panties, ever so gently inserting his fingers inside of me. I had only read about what happens between a man and a woman, but nothing told me about how it felt. Not even stealing a first kiss and a boob grope from a kid named Joey in my freshman year prepared me for this. I could feel a weird pressure building inside, and yet, it felt so good. It must have been right, I thought. He was my teacher, and I trusted in what he was teaching me.

He kept telling me how beautiful I was, confessing how he would think of me at night as he touched himself. He twistedly quoted Burns, *"And I will come again, my luve,"* as he finally overpowered me onto the cold, hard classroom floor and inserted his hardened cock into my virginal center. My feelings were mixed with shame and curiosity and confusion, but it felt so good that I didn't make him stop—even if it pained me in the beginning; it quickly turned pleasurable.

Whatever he was doing made my body rise and shudder into a maddening explosion. He then moaned my name—he really loved me!

And yet, as he pulled out of me and zipped up his

pants, he simply congratulated me on getting an "A" in his class, and threatened if I ever told anyone, he would make certain I would never graduate high school and that my parents would learn how much of a seductress whore I really was.

Deepen the black around the heart—the fire to singe an outline of the gentle love it's supposed to represent.

He left me on the cold floor in a panic, half of my clothes crumpled in a sinful ball in the corner. I feared him and believed him. I knew I couldn't breathe a word or he'd make good on his promise—the danger in his eyes told me so.

How could I possibly have told anyone, anyway? At that moment, the whole family was rallied around Meg, whose heart had just been completely shattered by the cheating Scotty. Scotty, who was like a brother to me. Who I confided in about everything, who promised that he would always be there for me. "I'll always watch out for you, little sis. You can count on it."

But no, when he abandoned Meg, he abandoned me, and I was left with no one to guide me through this confusion and degradation of my body and soul.

It became all about "poor Meg;" I didn't exist. *Meg, Meg, Meg.* We had to be gentle with her and kiss her ass until her heart healed. Mom and Dad and even Granny and Pops had to keep checking in on her and walk on eggshells while she transformed from sweet and creative to ambitious and selfish. All the while, I was invisible.

Mia had hopelessly been in love with her high school sweetheart, Kevin, and life was working out swimmingly for her, so she didn't need any support. She gave all her attention to Meg, too, trying to save her from herself. But me? Nothing more than, "How's school going, Marissa?"

and a blank stare as they all barely waited for my response.

I had no one to unload my burden on, and so, I internalized it and never spoke a word. Thank God he didn't get me pregnant that day. I was grateful for that small miracle, though it took two period cycles and countless false home stick tests before I could breathe a sigh of relief.

I did graduate, however, with the sick irony of Mr. Terrance being the chosen one to hand me my diploma.

Let's crack open a bit of the sky...

So, between the ill-intended poetry readings and the bastardized brother, my heart hardened to the concept of romance altogether. It was then that I spiraled into a world of sex, drugs and booze. It was then that I decided I would use my body for power and be the one in control of who, when and how. No one would ever use me again.

And I, along with my descent into trouble, went completely unnoticed. Eventually, I got my act together before I needed rehab or offed myself, but I never completely converted to "good girl" status, if you know what I mean. It wasn't until a few years later that I confided in Jay about all that went down, and he swore that my good old teacher was lucky he had already tragically passed away from a car accident, otherwise, he would have gone after him. But karma got to him first and spared Jay the lifetime prison sentence.

What made that old, stuffed down memory resurface? I wondered, recovering from the bitter reenactment in my brain.

Finished, I stared at my canvas in disbelief. It was hauntingly disconcerting, and yet, the best creation I thought I had ever imagined. It wasn't some prissy little landmark scene that people would smile at and wow over.

It was raw and purely from me. Unfiltered.

I never heard him come in.

"Did you just make that? It's—disturbingly stunning," gasped EJ, moving in closer now that I was aware of his presence. Embarrassed that my work had been seen by someone who owned his own art gallery, I quickly made up a few excuses to preserve my artistic dignity.

"I—I was just playing around. It's not what I usually do. I was just upset and venting it out with paint," I explained.

"Just playing? Maybe you should just play around more often. Tell me—what do you usually design?"

"Landscapes. Buildings. A few sculptures of creatures or symbols of where I've been or memories that mean something to me. Something that moves me."

"Sounds positively ordinary," he mock yawned. "Are you happy with that work?"

"Everyone seems to think it's pretty," I admitted.

"Marissa, the first rule of art is that you don't make it for others. You make it for yourself so that others can see themselves through you," he enlightened. "This piece is phenomenal. This is exactly what I would love to feature in my gallery. I don't want your Ireland drawings," he decided emphatically.

"I want more of this. I want more primal passion and emotion. This isn't just heartbreak—this is the destruction of love that forever changes our hearts to black. It's not the sappy love song we sing to ourselves to make us hopeful—it's our real pain and loss portrayed in a way that pulls at us. This is brilliance, Marissa."

I only sat there looking at him in stunned reverence for his words. I never thought in a million years someone could see into me and accept that I had a darkness. Or that expressing that very darkness through art would be worth anything.

"Thank you," I replied meekly.

"Now that I have given my blessing for you to be the artist you are meant to be," he said in a softer, more conversational tone, "do you want to talk about the inspiration behind this painting? Are you all right, cuz?"

"I am, thank you. This helped. Sometimes I tend to overdramatize situations in my life," I laughed, pointing at the drawing. "I had a stupid fight with my boyfriend and best friend last night, and they pissed me off. Nothing life shattering, either." I wasn't about to go into the much deeper wound that breathed the real darkness into the dragon's life. Even in death, Mr. Terrance's threat haunted my truth-telling abilities.

"Well, they should piss you off more often," he joked, giving me a light kiss on the forehead as he left me to my finishing touches and went off for his final day of business. "Take care of yourself, young one. See you tomorrow."

After enjoying a light lunch with my sisters at the villa, we packed up our bags for a day at the beach. Meg was feeling much better, and Mia had our whole itinerary planned. I was feeling lighter as well, as if all the anger had been pulled out of me and onto the canvas. Had I discovered a new kind of therapy?

Our destination was Puerto Olímpico, where the 1992 Olympics were held. Before settling down onto the sandy beach, we checked out the famous "recent" addition; evidently, the games revitalized the economy and changed the culture of the city by opening up its heart to its oceanic roots.

A new skyline was built, marked by two new skyscrapers, a sports marina, several docks and the now famous golden fish. Restaurants and nightclubs lined the strip—something we were game for checking out as evening fell.

But first, it would be a day of sun and sand—and apparently, topless old ladies and speedo-wearing men. Even Mia laughed that she felt more confident about herself after witnessing sagging, aged boobs and beer bellies strutting their stuff without care.

The water was sparkling and colder than I expected. The saltwater revitalized my body, washing away the residual anger and frustration over my current dilemma. I had several texts from Josh that I ignored, eventually turning off my phone completely to avoid any further annoyance. Thankfully, Jay had no idea he was on my shit list, too—he'd figure that out tomorrow when I stopped responding to him tonight, though.

They both wanted me to have a sister trip—so that's exactly what I planned on doing.

We spent the afternoon laying in the hot sun, people-watching (we even stopped covering our eyes at one point) and swimming. We just talked and laughed like we used to—no heavy conversations, just fun sister chats that made it feel like we were young kids again. I needed this uninterrupted time with them more than I realized.

The evening continued with an incredible dinner at one of the seaside restaurants. We couldn't resist each ordering different dishes so that we could try as much as possible—pan-seared monkfish with braised kale, roasted garbanzo beans and spicy tomato sauce; sea scallops topped with a creamy bacon and mushroom sauce with baby lima beans; and of course, Mia had to go all weird on us and order the grilled octopus with fried potatoes and salsa verde.

I was game to give it a try (gross) but Meg wanted nothing to do with it, claiming the smell of it was making her sick to her stomach. As an alternate, we selected grilled lamb chops in a walnut cream sauce, which was a fabulous choice. The waitress insisted that we also try the legendary crema Catalana for dessert: a variation of crème brûlée but infused with hints of orange, lemon and cinnamon.

I might even dare to say it was better than the traditional French classic.

Feeling the heat rise up from the wine intoxication over dinner, I coerced my sisters into letting me dance off my alcohol at one of the nearby clubs.

Ah, now this felt like home to me. The bump of the beat and the sizzle of the salsa. Losing myself in music was the only way I could release stress in a non-sexual manner. Okay, well, I still was sexual about it, but kept my clothes on at least.

I kept downing the drinks, as the Spanish men were ever so generous in buying me them…much harder cocktails than dinner wine. My sisters were evidently becoming impatient waiting for me to get my fill of the evening so we could head home. Maybe if they loosened up a bit and accepted a drink offer themselves, they wouldn't be such old ladies.

Besides, my new dance partner, Santiago, was great company to keep; they were free to leave. I was in good hands. Literally.

He pulled me in close gyration, his hands planted firmly on my ass as I grinded into his under-the-pants hardening cock. I loved the feeling of knowing I was turning a man on and encouraged the seductive dance. I soon felt his hot breath biting at my neck and his hoarse invitation to take me home.

Josh, who?

But of course, dear old Mia had to ruin my fun by pulling us away and telling my never-to-be lover that I was in a serious relationship and that it was time for us to go home. Ugh, I was so pissed at her.

The whole cab ride back I remember I was yelling at them. I'm not exactly sure what I was saying, but I think I let the secret out that I thought Meg was a condescending, pretentious bitch and Mia was a nosy goody two-shoes and that I was tired of their constant belittling of me. Or something like that.

I believe I also proclaimed I was pissed at both Josh and Jay, though I'm not sure if I told them why exactly. I did let them know I wasn't pleased with how they pulled me off of Santiago, and that if I needed to have sex with a Catalonian stranger to get back at the jerks, it was my call to make and not theirs.

Oh, and I think I may have also admitted that I was not alone in Ireland and Italy, like they thought, before I passed out.

7

My head fucking hurts, I thought as the sun's beams stung my eyes. *How did I even get here?*

Oh, right. My sisters put me into a cab and must have tucked me in quickly. I was still in last night's clothes and the remnants of mascara were all over the bleached white pillows. Cleaning that wasn't going to be much fun.

Neither would returning the texts from a frantic Josh and Jay, although both seem to have settled down shortly after two a.m. when I saw the group text from Mia saying I was fine, just having too much fun. I'll have to remember to thank her for covering for me later.

Although I don't recall much, I figured I'd have some apologizing to do as well. I was not looking forward to the aftermath of my drunken stupor. I decided to prolong it as much as possible by hiding under the covers until the throbs went away. I could really use a joint right about now.

The peace didn't last long, as both of my sisters showed up at my bedroom door—one with a bottle of aspirin and the other with a huge jug of water.

"How's the hangover?" asked Mia.

"Terrible. I guess I deserve it after last night," I looked up apologetically.

"Oh, you do," replied Meg. "Sorry. I figured it would be okay for me to point it out since I'm the insufferable bitch of the family," she jabbed.

"Yeah, about that. There's a lot that is a blur, but I know I said some things I shouldn't have. I'm sorry."

Mia shot Meg a look that said "quit it" before turning back to me.

"We'll talk. Why don't you take a shower and then meet us at the pool when you're ready? EJ will join us later this afternoon, but us girls can have a little chat beforehand. Okay?"

Nodding my head in agreement and humiliation, I drank down three pills before getting out of the bed. I wasn't looking forward to the impending lecture from my sister-moms, but being stuck in a foreign country with no way out, I guess I couldn't run away from my own mouth this time.

"I am really sorry for everything I said last night," I began, approaching my two sisters sitting on the deep-cushioned lounges, leaving one in the middle that obviously was meant for me. Great, a Marissa sandwich. This was going to be hell.

Thank goodness Meg seemed to have cooled down a bit, probably thanks to Mia's interference—though my level-headed sister wasn't exactly in a happy-go-lucky state of mind herself.

"First, let's start with how you really feel about us," prompted Mia, like a damn kindergarten school teacher starting her lesson after morning circle time.

"I know I said mean things, but I don't know exactly what I said. I'm guessing from your comment this morning, Meg, that I was pretty nasty to you," I began.

"I didn't realize I was such a horrible sister, always making you feel bad about yourself," she answered in a saddened, remorseful voice.

"I know I can be challenging," I admitted. "But yes, sometimes you make me feel like I am not good enough to even be your sister. I should have come to you about this before, and not waited until I was drunk."

"There are a lot of things we should have talked about before, but yes—having an open and honest relationship with each other would be a great start," she acknowledged. "I accept that I am not the kindest or most sensitive of sisters. I haven't always been there for you, and I'm sorry if I've ever made you feel like I didn't love you.

"I do love you with all my heart. We may not always see eye to eye little sis, but make no mistake that my intentions are never to hurt you. My job is to protect you and look out for you. But I promise to make more of an effort to listen instead of judge."

"Deep down, I know that. And I know how impossible I can be sometimes. I promise that instead of reacting or getting all jealous, I will try harder to open up about what I am feeling. I don't want us to always be fighting, Meg."

My eldest sister moved to pull me into her arms with tears in her eyes. "Me neither, Mar. Let's start over?"

"Absolutely," I smiled big and squeezed her tighter.

"And I can't help being the peacemaker of the family, but this is why," Mia pointed out.

"I know you mean well, too. I just wish you weren't so cynical or question everything I do," I shared.

"I guess we all have parts of our nature that we can't help," she chuckled. "But if we just accept these parts of each other, and respect how we feel, I think we can navigate this sister thing much better. We have a wonderful bond—one that I never want to break."

"I agree," said Meg. "I don't ever want to lose what we have. You both mean too much to me."

"To me, too. I'd be lost without you. Thanks for being so understanding. My big mouth and impulsive actions have a habit of ruining a lot of things in my life."

"About that," Meg initiated. "You said a lot of inaudible things last night about being angry at both Jay and Josh. And you also mentioned confiding in Jay about some note. What's that all about?"

Fuck. I really do have loose lips when I drink. No use in hiding it from them now.

"Okay, but please don't get mad at me."

"We won't," Mia reassured me as she tossed a glance over to Meg to beg for her new oath of patience with me.

"A few days before we left, I received a new threatening note in my mailbox that said 'Watch your back. I'm not done with you bitches yet.'"

"Why didn't you tell us?" Mia gently asked.

"I was afraid that you both would cancel this trip and I'd never get my statue." I had to be honest. This wasn't a game and they did have a right to know what was going on. I couldn't choke down the truth anymore. It's never served me well before.

"It was wrong of me. I get that now."

"Does anyone know except Jay?"

"No. I lied to Josh and said it was just a thank you note from EJ and Rodney. In that moment, I didn't need him jumping to conclusions and freaking out on me. He's so overprotective. I didn't want to tell you and worry you both, either. It was only the one note, and I haven't gotten anything else since. Except—"

"Except what?" probed Mia.

"Except at our last family dinner, when Bruce was alone with me in the kitchen, he said those same exact words to me: 'Watch your back.' It threw me off, wondering if he was behind the note. Knowing that Josh and Bruce already had their reservations about each other, I didn't want to tell Josh just yet.

"I happened to be over at Jay's and we were talking, and something made me want to tell him. I knew that he would keep an eye on our family while we were away, in exchange for me keeping him posted every night." I saw Mia hold up a hand to Meg, who I could tell wanted to make a comment about my loose lips with Jay about our personal family business.

"So, nothing else has happened except the note and cryptic conversation with Bruce? Nothing at all in Spain?" Mia wanted to clarify.

"Absolutely nothing. I promise you."

"Okay, that's a relief. We'll still want to alert the guards and let them know of potential danger. I think just to be safe, Mia should call Kevin and let him know about your exchange with Bruce. Let's have him casually keep an eye on things. He can be discreet." We all nodded in agreement.

"I understand why you didn't tell us before, but if anything else happens, will you please, please let us know?" Meg pleaded.

"I will. I shouldn't have kept it from you. I'm really sorry."

"Now, why are you fighting with both Josh and Jay? Does it have to do with any of this?" Meg continued her questioning. Wow, I really did say a lot last night. What else did I divulge?

"So, Josh saw Bruce and Jay at my regular coffee shop the other day. He thought it was suspicious and informed me that I was not to talk to Jay anymore until he figured it out. Like I would do that," I rolled my eyes in remembrance of his stupid demand.

"And then I tried to find out what Jay was doing that day, to see if he'd just tell me and give me a logical explanation—especially since they've never met before. But he never admitted to being with Bruce, so now I know he is keeping something from me and that ticks me off."

"Men," Meg mused. "They really are primeval creatures."

"Well, maybe after today, you can smooth things over with them. You are going through a lot right now—these journeys are more intense than you can even imagine. You are in a foreign country, and not only is it physically tiring, but mentally and emotionally challenging.

"As frustrated as you are with both of them, try to keep things balanced until you get home and can have one-on-one conversations with them both—like you just had with us," Mia suggested.

"You're right," I conceded. "I'll make peace by the end of today. But first, I'm starving. I need to eat something and then I would really love to talk to EJ—about anything except my life and drunken blabberings."

"Okay, we'll reserve the 'I wasn't alone in Ireland and Italy' conversations for another time then," winked Meg. My God, I was never going to drink again.

EJ's entrance to the rooftop pool was nothing short of ostentatious, with his loud flamingo shirt, khaki shorts and wide-brimmed sun hat announcing his arrival before his booming voice did. Someone was ready for a fiesta with his tray of delicious snacks and refreshing drinks (non-alcoholic, mercifully).

"Who's ready for a little mid-day grub?"

"Perfect timing, EJ. I'm absolutely starving," I proclaimed with gratitude as I grabbed some ham and cheese and a few pieces of bread and started shoving the food into my mouth.

"Mmm-hmm. I thought you would be, little señorita salsa."

"Does everybody know?" The red rushed right to my cheeks.

"Well, honey, I was here when they brought you in. Who do you think was able to carry your plastered patootie into the bedroom?"

"Oh. Thank you."

"Not a problem, cuz. You are turning out to be quite entertaining. I like you," he said as he poked my nose with his finger with a little "boop"-like noise. I couldn't help but laugh at this character. Should I tell him he was equally entertaining?

"Now then. Everything has been set up with your statue. It's currently going through an appraisal and validation and it should be ready for you to claim the day after tomorrow."

"Wow, that was fast. Usually we have to jump through multiple hoops to get there," said Meg.

"Well, I've been doing the hoop-jumping, so you're welcome," he responded with a smile and mimicked the scoring of a basket. "Marissa will just have to show her identification and get fingerprinted, but it should be relatively easy after that. I'll take you down myself to make sure it's smooth as peanut butter."

"Thank you for everything you have done for us," Mia said gratefully.

"Aw, shucks, it's nothing. I'm tickled y'all are my cousins. I've enjoyed getting to know you. I don't have any other family, other than Rodney and his kin, and this new cousin Teresa here. It's nice to know I actually have local relations."

"We feel the same way," I promised him. "So, how is it that we are so intimately connected when our lines are so many generations apart and scattered? It makes sense to us about the O'Sullivans and Bianchi families, but how is it that our Rubio roots are so easily traced?"

"Ah, that my dear, is a wonderful story. You see, when Elena went off to marry Banan, that was not the end of her family ties with her brother and mother. Quite the contrary," he began.

He proceeded to explain how Elena and Eduardo kept in touch, and how while James O'Sullivan was still alive, he would make arrangements to bring his daughter-in-law back to Spain to see her family at least once or twice a year. He really embraced Elena into the family, and by extension, her family.

Their mother had fallen quite ill, and with Eduardo a struggling middle class fisherman trying to provide for his own family of four, James had sent money over for her care. Eventually, he brought their mother to Ireland where Elena could care for her herself until her passing.

The Rubios never forgot the kindness of the O'Sullivans, and so, EJ's grandfather, Juan Tomás (and to some extent, his brother, Miguel), continued the kinship down the line as Cian and Banan Junior's cousins.

Junior didn't care so much for this Spanish family, but Cian was always welcoming and kept in touch. Juan Tomás made a trip out to Ireland upon Lena's birth, bringing along his only son, Matteo, who was nearing adulthood.

Matteo had big dreams of moving to America, as did

Cian. And so, Cian and Juan Tomás forged an agreement that Matteo could indeed make a life for himself in America, under the care of Cian and Alessia. When the little O'Sullivan family departed, Matteo hugged his parents goodbye and set off to fulfill his dream.

After only two years, Matteo was then of age and ready to move out on his own. He had grown quite fond of his baby cousin, Lena, and was the one person in the entire country who looked out for her welfare, even years after her parents died and she was stuck in a loveless marriage with Antonio Marino.

Lena and Matteo kept in touch, though time and circumstances widened the distance between them, most of it due to the controlling nature of the Marinos. But of course, the spirit that resided in Lena wanted to continue honoring the only family connection she had, and so her son, Leigh, and Matteo's son, EJ—a few decades apart in age—knew of each other from brief visits and a few stories passed down.

It's why it was so easy for Leigh to track down EJ after Lena revealed all of this family history.

"So, how does the dragon statue come into play?" I was dying to know more.

"Okay, little minx, I will tell you a little bit about it since you have very little patience," he chided. "Forgive me, cousin Leigh, but I'm going to have to bend a few rules for this one over here," he continued as he raised his hands in prayer to the clouds.

"As I mentioned the other day, when Horace disgraced the family, all that was left to him was this dragon statue from his mother. Well, when he killed himself and it was found among his possessions, it naturally went to his only son. Although my great-uncle Miguel was better suited for it philosophically—God rest his soul, the manipulative philanderer—Eduardo thought it would be in better hands with my grandfather.

"Miguel really couldn't care less about it, so gratefully, there was no objection to it continuing down the line to my father as he left for America, so that he would have a piece of his family with him always. He then granted it to me as his only child, where I held it in high regard at my gallery until I received the call from Leigh.

"Lena had told him about the relic, and he wanted to know if I would be open to passing it across the lines to his youngest granddaughter. Being that I have no children of my own, and I hadn't known about Teresa at that point in time, I had no qualms about handing it off—especially after hearing him talk about you. It was meant for you, darling," he added.

"I'm not sure I understand why," I said, rather offended by the whole idea of it.

"My dear, why is that?"

"You just said it was passed to your grandfather, but his brother, who was not quite so upstanding, was actually more deserving of the statue? That doesn't exactly make me feel like my grandfather had a high opinion of me."

"Oh my. Oh, no, no, no. You have me all wrong, cuz. I can't get into the meaning behind the statue just yet. But I can tell you there was more to Miguel that made him a better match. Let's just say passion is involved, and a wonderful life lesson. Do not jump to lopsided conclusions just yet, until you hear the whole story," he gently lectured.

"Once you learn about the dragon in a few days, it will all make sense to you. But little one, you must know that your grandfather was quite taken with you. I assure you, this was skillfully coordinated, and after meeting you, I can attest that the man knew exactly what he was doing."

"Okay. I guess I will just have to wait, huh?"

"Indeed," he affirmed. "But—I do have an idea that I think will help you pass the time. How would you like to take a trip to Madrid?"

"That would be incredible!" exclaimed Meg. "Can we go see some flamenco dancers?"

Mia chimed in. "Oh, I'd love to see the Buen Retiro Park if we could! I've read so much about it."

"Yes, yes," he laughed as we all came at him. "We can do all that. But the main attraction will be the Prado Museum. A little birdy told me that Marissa's favorite artist is Goya. Now, how can she come to Spain and not see the grandest displays of his work?"

"Are you serious? Are you freaking serious?" I couldn't believe it. EJ was the best cousin ever!

"I'm serious! It's a 3-hour train ride, so to make the most of the day, it's best that we're ready to head out by three o'clock. If we plan this right, we can arrive in time to check into our hotel and then grab a flamenco dinner show this evening."

I ran over to him and embraced him with the biggest hug I had ever given someone. "Thank you from the bottom of my heart."

Before we left, I decided to follow my sisters' advice and restore peace to my relationships with Josh and Jay. I texted them both individually, letting them know we were doing well, had no troubles and were headed on an overnight trip to Madrid. I figured this short exchange would be enough to patch things up temporarily.

Well, with Jay, it was easy, because he never knew I was mad at him to begin with, thanks to Mia's intervention last night. As for Josh, his response was a cool *"have fun"* and not much else, but he did sign it with his signature *"J xo,"* so that was at least promising.

Guess he knows I need time to cool off, yet appreciates the fact that I reached out and acknowledged him. I'll deal with my relationship issues another time.

Tonight, we were going to leave everything behind us and enter into the exotic world of flamenco. Happening upon a local Madrid hotspot for both dinner and a show after checking into the hotel, the music took control and I immediately felt alive again.

The food was outstanding as we dined on a tasting menu of scallop carpaccio, wild sea bass, roasted pigeon and lamb with pumpkin purée and a side of buckwheat risotto and roasted vegetables. I refrained from drinking, as did Meg, but EJ and Mia certainly enjoyed their share of the wine pairings that accompanied our gourmet cuisine.

Watching the flamenco dancers was a complete sensory overload in the most wonderful of ways, from the vibrant costumes and masterful movements of the dancers, singers and guitar players, to the mesmerizing music that simply moved our souls. Our Spain experience certainly would not have been complete without this cultural extravaganza.

I'm not sure what it was, but I felt the pull to Madrid to be even stronger than that to Barcelona. The coastal town—and especially its outskirt town, Sitges, where we were staying—were both truly magnificent, no question. But there was an aura, a magnetism that was luring me into the core of Madrid's very existence.

Even the Buen Retiro Park we went to in the morning

felt different from the other natural landmarks we've seen over the last few months. There was a magic and grace to it—even though, yes, it had lakes and monuments and gorgeous fountains like all the rest, but the ambiance was unexpectedly enticing.

The walkways were expertly manicured with the brightest symmetrical greenery. I even found myself enamored by the Crystal Palace, with its unique metal and glass architecture that self-reflected into a lake.

But what I loved most were the daring sculptures—one in particular called *El Retiro,* or Fallen Angel. It is said to be the likeness of Satan, the only one of its kind, his fall depicted as he is surrounded by demon heads. It was defiantly fascinating.

We elected to sit among the open-air gardens for a fun picnic lunch, which Mia, of course, had arranged for us on her early trip to a local market with EJ. She hadn't been able to do as much cooking on this trip, so we indulged her request to pull together a special meal for us. She didn't disappoint.

The morning was light and relaxing, yet my nerves were getting worked up. I felt butterflies in anticipation of finally getting to seeing Goya's work in the flesh—or stone, as it may be.

The experience was more than I could have ever imagined.

I have to say, even as magnificent as my art experience has been so far on these three trips, nothing was as dreamlike as finally being able to see the works of my favorite artist of all time.

Known for capturing the darkness of mankind, I couldn't help but be drawn into the realities of his vision and feel his pain. It was as if I somehow related to the misery he exposed, wishing he could bring the internal darkness within me to such beautiful, expressive light.

Sure, some find him sadistic and crazy. I admit that there are some disturbing pieces, and yet, what he depicts is truth. Even in his *Black Paintings* of other worldly gods and creatures, they represent the human plight and angst.

Why did I feel so guilty for being fascinated by the darkness? For hearing the call? Sensing my internal dilemma, EJ found a way to my side where he could speak without my sisters overhearing.

"I see you are completely captivated, my cousin. Does that trouble you?"

"Yes. I mean, so much of his work depicts violence and brutality, and yet, I feel like I truly *get* it; that I live it. Like it's not that I just understand the artist's interpretation, but also the subjects within and their own drive to commit such savagery. Does that make me, I don't know, evil?" I looked at him with imploring eyes, surprised at myself for revealing such a personal inner secret to someone I barely knew.

"No, cuz, it does not. It makes you emotionally connecting and passionate. Tell me—what is it that moves you so much about his work?" he asked, genuinely interested and non-judgmental.

"Human beings can be ugly and cruel, and it doesn't make the world a better place by living in denial. At least, not in my opinion. Sex, drugs, war, crime—we are that as much as we are hope, faith and love. When we embrace the very idea that we each have a dark side to us, we are that much closer to living in our own truth."

"Indeed. And, therein, lies the beauty of *el dragón,*" he cryptically hinted and walked away to join the others, while I pondered what he could possibly mean by that.

8

The trip back to Sitges was uneventful; mostly a foursome of sleepyheads finally getting some rest after a long day's excursion. We all instantly retreated to our bedrooms to continue the slumber, knowing that tomorrow was the big day. I'd finally have my hands on my statue, and hopefully the reveal of my connection to it.

Of course, I couldn't sleep. I stared at the ceiling for hours trying to figure out what the dragon meant, and what the "theme" of this journey would be for me. Love for Meg, dreams for Mia. So far, all I experienced was a fascination for obscurity and fighting with a whole bunch of loved ones.

Simply confirmation that I was a black sheep? Or rather, a flame-breathing dragon?

This shadowy ewe knew she had to make some kind of amends with Josh, so I called him. It was just approaching evening back in New York, so I knew he would be awake. As expected, he was colder than a polar bear in the Arctic Ocean.

"How was your trip to Madrid?" *Great,* I thought sarcastically. We'd go the small talk route.

"Unbelievable," I barely answered. "Listen, Josh—"

"No, wait Marissa," he cut me off. "I've had a lot of time to think, and I realized it was unfair of me to ask you to stop speaking to Jay. I just get so jealous of the guy," he admitted, melting his iceberg tone as he got right to the point.

"Thank you for saying that. But you have no reason to be jealous of him, Josh. I love *you.*"

"I love you, too."

"I'm sorry, too, for overreacting. I know you are just trying to protect me. I'm trying to accept that there is someone in my life who truly loves me. It's a struggle, like I'm waiting for this 'too good to be true' scenario to fall apart in my face and it scares the fuck out of me. So, I default to pushing you away before you can do it to me.

"Classic Marissa," I explained, feeling the need to pour my heart out instead of shut him out.

"I know, and I tried to give you space without being angry. But I'm a hothead, too," he laughed. "I guess we both just need to accept that about each other—but also learn how to trust and communicate better instead of blow up. Can you forgive me for being a caveman?"

"If you can forgive me for being an unrelenting firecracker, then sure," I giggled. "But please, don't give me masked ultimatums like that ever again. We may be together, but I will always be an independent woman and I won't do well to be controlled."

"Understood. I will not chain you up like that again," he said sincerely.

"Well, I didn't say you couldn't chain me up," I replied seductively, leading us to a more pleasant bedtime conversation.

After a sexually releasing make-up video chat, I thought I should quickly text Jay as promised before I fell asleep. Maybe now that a few days had passed, he might be more willing to offer up the information about seeing

Bruce. And I knew exactly how to get it out of him.

Just got back from Madrid. 1 might need to live here. All is quiet though. How are things over there?

Hey beautiful. 1 had a feeling you would love Madrid. Things here are great but lonely. 1 miss you.

Miss you too. How's my family? Been keeping an eye on them and Bruce?

Everyone is fine. Just like 1 promised.

Have you seen them?

Kevin had questions so 1 stopped by Mia's house to check on them. They suckered me into tea time lol. But they are doing great. No worries.

Is that all?

Yeah. Why?

No reason. K TTYT.

Okay...good night Riss. xo

I didn't even bother to respond. He just failed my little test. No mention of meeting up with Bruce. Either something was wrong and he wasn't telling me, or he was up to something. I hated being across the ocean because typically, I'd show up at his doorstep and demand an answer.

But as my sisters suggested, I'm trying to keep a cool head and bide my time until I can confront him in person and get the real truth. Easy for them to say, but I knew I wasn't going to get it over a text or even a phone call. We all group chatted with Mom, Granny and the kids while we were at the park, and everyone was sincerely well, so I could believe that at least.

Finally feeling the sleep set in, I allowed my body to sink down into the soft covers and enter dreamland. Though, with visions of bloodshed, dragon fire and destruction, I'm not exactly sure I could call it that.

Needless to say, I did not wake up refreshed and perky like Mia. The remnants of the nightmares were disturbing as I adjusted to a new day. Instead of joining my family for breakfast, I snuck a cup of black coffee and a piece of toast on my way up to the studio. I had some images that wanted to leave my head and fill up a canvas. I guess there were more wounds that needed artistic therapy.

This time, the sun was the victim. Set amongst a picturesque, bright blue sky with cirrus-type clouds above a sparkling waterfall, it was torn. Claws from an unidentified creature's scaly hand had ripped through its fiery surface to reveal drippings of black blood that melded with the flow of the natural water source, creating alternate waves of sparkle and dullness.

I wanted to scar the fake brightness of its omnipotent beams, representing the idea that everything has a dark and a light side. Not even the most perfect object in all the universe is immune to the grasp of the shadows.

No, not even the flawless Megan Rossi or sugary sweet Mia Logan. I saw their hidden darkness, yet others just saw them as perfection. I'm not sure why these feelings resurfaced when we had all just bonded and reconnected. Where were these emotions coming from? I thought we had come to an understanding, and yet, I could still feel the resentment over the attention they got while I was always pushed to the side. I had to do my feelings justice and let them be drawn.

The conversation with EJ about how we are all light and dark kept coming back to me as I poured my soul into the painting. I felt driven to convey the message that alluded me in words but found its place in color. The madness had to have its say.

Looking at the hasty work I just procured within only an hour, I was stunned at how pleased I was with it. Like I had channeled the madness from somewhere beyond my consciousness, even as thoughts ran rampant. That idea terrified me—*am I possessed by some wicked power somehow?*

Knowing my imagination was sprinting a marathon, I covered up the canvas with a sheet and headed down the stairs to get ready for the day. I took a deep breath, feeling some relief that my sisterly competition in my mind had been released onto the canvas. I had more important emotions to confront.

Today, EJ was going to reveal more details about the statue and how to get it. By evening, it would be in my hands.

With guards in tow and back at the villa to protect us, we traveled into Barcelona to a small alleyway antique store, where a fat, balding, jovial old man came waddling over to us with a big, silly grin for EJ. He signaled to wait a moment until he was done with the only customer in the store, and then locked the front door and put up his "closed" sign.

"Bienvenido, Eduardo," then turning to shake each of our hands, *"Es maravilloso conocerlas señoritas.* I am honored to finally meet you. I am Señor Guarez. Please, come sit down."

We sat upon the red velvet-like cushioned couches in a small lounge area of the store while he disappeared into the back to retrieve a stack of paperwork and a black wooden box. After checking my identification and fingerprints, he motioned over to EJ for a final confirmation.

"For you, Señorita Rossi," Señor Guarez said as he finally handed me my intended heirloom. Inside this box was what I'd been waiting for, for close to six months. I couldn't breathe; the anticipation was building up like rising ecstasy not wanting its release just yet.

I had an image in my mind, but nothing prepared me for the grandeur that was placed into my hands. This had to be the greatest orgasm of my life.

Possibly about a foot or so in height, the double-headed black dragon stood proudly defending its mountainous post upon a base of clean, solid black marble. Its single body twisted with smooth, yet edgily defined body scales with swirls of white embedded within the natural stone. The tail majestically lay curved upon the base, a single sparkling diamond upon its pointy tip.

The right head—the demon side I supposed—had a red eyeball and a gorgeous matching blaze of fire spewing out, as its corresponding hand reached out to grab something within the ethers in front of it. The left side possessed a dark, but lovely blue eye that looked towards the sky with a less intimidating light yellow flame and its claw reaching upwards.

The appraiser stopped me mid-thought to explain some of its unique composition.

"The dragon itself was sculpted entirely from black onyx. You can see here the natural white and gray hues buried within it. Stunning piece of rock. This here is a rounded ruby eye and his flame was shaped using a red fire opal. The artist had a love of rich colors and materials," he illuminated, happy to show off his historian expertise.

"If you look closely, you can see the way this piece was created, that it was shaped and intricately bonded into layers. Underneath here is a solid copper tongue. Blink and you'd miss it! The other side has a princess cut sapphire eye and her flame is made entirely from citrine with a gold tongue underneath."

"That's my birthstone," I recollected as I explored every inch of the statue, lingering on the yellow stone flame that I knew so well. Thoughtfully, I considered what he had just said. "Him and her?"

"Yes, him and her, simply like yin and yang, light and dark. Polar opposites that can come together as one. It is how the creator himself described it," he explained.

"Goya?"

"It is believed to be so, yes. Legend has it that when the art world was creating sculptures of people and religious symbols, his work was way too ominous to be accepted—at first. A double-headed dragon? Blasphemy, as it represented pure evil in a timeworn Spanish era. Society was not ready for such things.

"Eventually, as we all know, Goya made his name anyway in the world. But this being his first sculpted piece, as it is said, it held such a special significance that he never again offered it up as part of his collection.

"It originally did not have this detailed gem work; only solid bronze and brass flames, from what I have been told. He crafted those exquisite gems later in life as he made his fortune and perfected this magnum opus of his heart," he added as an aside.

"There is a deep story behind its creation, and how it came to be passed to your family, but your cousin is the one with that information, not I. But after studying this, I can assure you, it is very much in line with his beginning personal stylings. It is a Goya," he confirmed.

We all turned to EJ at that moment, who aloofly gave his "not now" look, I think rather relishing the fact that he was keeping us in suspense. We thanked Señor Guarez, placing the statue gently back into its case as I signed off on the paperwork and made our way to the car.

"It's gorgeous, Mar. The whole piece seems to suit you," Meg commented on the drive back.

"You think so?"

"Absolutely. It's got that edginess that's uniquely you, yet sparkles with beauty. I think a boring ring or wooden box would not have spoken to you the way this did today," she considered. Wow, I was beginning to realize my sister did understand me after all.

"Is that how you see me?"

"It's how I've always seen you," she smiled. "It's a good thing," she added, I think hoping that she wasn't offending me. She didn't at all, though.

She was one hundred percent right. It did speak to me, just like Goya's other paintings and sculptures, but more on a personal level as I held it in my own hands. I let my eyes wander through its complicated details as my fingers moved across its multi-textural terrain.

"So, what does this all mean for Marissa?" asked Mia on my behalf.

"That has yet to be revealed," EJ gently cautioned. "I know you are anxious to know the story, but the dragon will reveal itself to you first."

"What do you mean?" I asked, puzzled.

"Well, I think you should take some time to sit with it. Ask it what message it has for you," he offered.

"You want me to talk to a statue?"

He burst out laughing at my sassy tone.

"Yes, I want you to talk to a statue. Actually, better yet—just like your sisters did for their adventures, I think it would be a good idea for you to take a few days to yourself to really reflect on your journey and what you've learned.

"You are to embark on a quest of self-discovery. Sitting in the presence of this superb piece of art might give you some of the answers you are seeking." *That's funny,* I thought to myself, *I wasn't aware I had any questions, other than the symbolism of this dang thing.*

"Where would I go?"

"You can stay here," Mia proposed. "Meg and I were talking about this after we tucked you in the other night. We are so close to France that we thought we could hop on the train and visit some of the southern areas while we are here.

"And even though you'd have time to yourself, we'd also feel more comfortable knowing at the end of the night, EJ was still in the house with you. You know, just in case."

"And the villa is big enough for me to stay well out of your way," he agreed. "I could use some downtime myself for a few days."

"Okay," I relented, knowing how much I hated being alone. At least I'd have the presence of EJ if the solitude got to be too much. Josh wasn't due to arrive for a few more days, and I would've liked that time with him, but with the speed in which my sisters planned their escape, it looked like I wasn't being left with a choice.

"There is one more thing I would like to share with you all first, though, if you have a moment this evening," he said as he pulled up to the villa. "Meet me for dinner on the second floor terrace in about an hour and we can discuss," he directed.

We did as requested, walking into a neatly set table for four featuring gazpacho soup bowls and a Mediterranean mixed green salad that EJ picked up from a local takeout eatery. He took no time getting down to business.

"The reason I have called this little assembly this evening is to give you some insight into the grand finale," he previewed.

"Although Marissa's journey is not over quite yet, there is a bigger picture that has yet to be unveiled. I believe Sorella Maria alluded to the jewelry box being more than it appears?"

"Yes," Mia responded. "She mentioned something about needing to figure out how to unlock it, but I have yet to discover how. But I do hear the rattling inside, so if something got in there, there's a way to get it out."

"There is indeed," he shared. "This is your final task. You must find the map that gives you the instructions on how to locate the keys and where to insert them."

"A map?" Meg inquired. "Where would we even look?"

"That part I can tell you," he grinned. "It is within the dragon statue. Find the map, and you can unravel the mystery."

"I thoroughly inspected every inch of that statue. Nothing is hidden in there," I protested.

"Just like life, not everything is easily accessible at our fingertips. It will take clever thinking and determination to find the loophole," he advised.

"Do you know where it is? I mean, I know we are the ones who have to find it, but were you told?" asked Mia.

"I was," he acknowledged. "You see, a lot of planning went into this whole legacy journey than you even realize," he began.

"When Leigh conjured up this plan, he left no stone unturned. He began with what he knew from his mother and went to work to contact each of us—Colleen, Sorella Maria and myself. His first step was to actually make sure the heirlooms existed and that they were safe, preserved and contained their original heritage letters."

Sensing my next question, he added, "I do have yours, Marissa. But my instructions were to wait for the right time to give it to you. And I will, I promise."

"After I talk to the double dragon head," I replied sarcastically, causing him to guffaw grandly.

"Yes, yes," he replied. "Oh, how I adore your sass, young one."

"Continuing on. Once the three of us confirmed that the pieces were all intact as desired, he summoned us to meet in Florence—Francesco as well. Leigh chose this location because of Sorella Maria's inability to travel far, and also because that's where the jewelry box, with all its intriguing secrets, was held.

"We were just as enthralled by the mystery of it all as you were—unending questions and desires to know the scandals and riddles behind it. He indulged us, sharing every last juicy detail. Admittedly, we each knew pieces of it already; but Leigh had the links that connected it all together.

"Even though the three of us do not have our own lines to pass it down to, the fact that we were included and learned such a robust, magical, inspiring family tree was worth more than the riches these tokens we bestow upon you bring.

"It was his hope that through the three of you, the full stories would be carried on. In fact, Meg, he wished for you to author the complete legacy, you being the writer of the family."

"What? But I thought this was to remain a secret? For family only?" she disputed.

"And that is where the ingenuity of your grandfather comes in. You weave the story of truth and present it to the world as fiction. Only within your bloodlines will they know the fairy tale is a reality."

I saw the epiphany dawning upon my sister's face, and an excited glow about her. Like a life purpose had just awakened within her soul. I could tell she couldn't wait for time alone to begin writing it all out; it wasn't unlike my desire to paint at the exact moment of inspiration. Another likeness I hadn't considered.

"The jewelry box can in fact be opened, my dear hearts. I have seen it. That is why Leigh brought us all together. Leigh had the map from his mother, who held it in her safekeeping. No one could come across that map and have any idea what it was or where to find the pieces—that is the deliciousness of it all.

"It was so strategically planned by your great-grandmother, to be carried out by your grandfather in the end. In fact, it was Lena who created the chest as a puzzle box; it was not designed that way originally. She took great care in converting it from the traditional open box format—which is why you can see the seal along its side, but it is welded shut."

Mia nodded her head in awe and acknowledgment, knowing she had painstakingly scrutinized that chest even more than I did the statue.

"Lena worked with an expert lockbox maker in

Florence—when she was off on a 'ladies retreat' upstate, or so her husband thought. She made sure her actions could not be traced for fear of the Marinos uncovering the truth of her wealth.

"Before heading to Florence, she had already started making the plans to reclaim the family treasures and ensure their authenticity and legacy preservation. She then headed to Florence where a trusted woodworker, an old friend of Sorella Maria's, took her creative vision for the puzzle box and brought it to life.

"She had him draw the map, which he also carefully built into the dragon statue, and then she clandestinely returned all of the different tokens to the current owners— Colleen, Sorella Maria and my father, Matteo—with the prediction that her son or his heirs would one day be the ones to carry on the legacy.

"She planted the seeds. It was hard for any of us not to help Leigh harvest the crops when he finally reached out. To this day, it amazes me the foresight that Lena had. But then again, growing up with a mother who practiced 'witchcraft,'" he said playfully, gesturing with quotation mark fingers, "none of us should be surprised by her intuitive abilities."

"That really is something," Meg said softly, just as taken aback by the story as we were. But EJ had more to say.

"When Leigh was with us, it was the first time he or any of us was able to see how the box opened, and it was flawlessly inspiring. Lena, for all her broken-hearted faults, was a genius. We found a beautiful note written in her handwriting to her future generations, which we read with tears in our eyes before placing it back inside.

"That is also when Leigh added his own surprise

inheritance gifts that would await his true family, as he called all of you, upon its grand opening.

"That is why we have summoned all of the cousins and your mother and grandmother and children to come join us, because it is about more than just you three. It is about family and a woman who loved so deeply, she deserved a distinguished affair in her honor.

"I hope that I have left you inspired enough to find the map. For once you find it, it will be up to you to decode the different keys and figure out how to solve the puzzle. This mission, should you accept it, will unlock a life-altering future for you all."

9

After our dramatic evening of storytelling, we decided to postpone the map search for a few days while we went on our own; we'd reconvene when my sisters returned, though I'm not sure I could be patient enough to avoid looking for it in their absence.

Meg and Mia were traveling before daybreak and early bird EJ decided he was headed to the beach, leaving me to figure out how in the hell I was going to spend my day alone.

I figured I could go back to one of those museums and enjoy the artwork without pressure. But then I realized that nothing would compare to the greatness I experienced in Madrid, so visiting a different kind of landmark in Barcelona might be a better idea.

I started out at the Boqueria Market, famous for its hundreds of fresh fruit and vegetable stands and more. *Mia would love this place,* I thought to myself as I sipped on a freshly squeezed juice smoothie. I could only imagine the meal she would concoct for us from the colorful ingredients that lined the street.

Walking around the area, I came upon the Gran Teatre del Liceu, where they just so happened to have a rare morning opera performance. Although I figured this was more of Meg's thing than mine, I decided to give it a chance. After all, I was here to experience as much as I could on this journey, and I really didn't know how else to spend my time.

I did not expect the show to move me so much; I couldn't understand a word, and yet, the emotions made their way into my heart and my eyes. The tears streamed down my face as I tragically watched the actress's love of her life die in her arms. Was I becoming a—gasp—*romantic?*

Shaking that scary notion off, I continued to wander down Las Ramblas, the bustling boulevard EJ had taken us to on our first night. *Oh yeah,* I remembered, as I walked towards the Erotic Museum. *Now, that's more my style.*

It wasn't at all what I expected—not lewd or distasteful in the least. And it wasn't full-on pornography-laden like a strip club or sex store, either. Rather, the museum was a historical depiction of sex throughout the centuries. Quite fascinating to enter the worlds of Kama Sutra and Japanese sculptures—even Picasso works were on display!

The visuals, although treasured pieces of art, did arouse me as I walked through the nude photos, sculptures with oversized penises and orgy-like paintings. Fuck, why couldn't Josh be here right now to take care of my sexual needs?

I wandered into a less crowded alleyway to give him a call, but received his automated text that he was in court for the day and would return my (anyone's) message at his earliest convenience.

So much for that idea, I pouted. Knowing I needed to distract myself, I strolled on down to a nearby café for a pitcher of sangria and some tapas. At least if I got myself into trouble, my sisters weren't there to rat me out.

No such luck. Turns out, there weren't many prospects—

at least, not mid-week—as many Barcelonans were set to return to their jobs for the afternoon. A bit tipsy, I boarded a train back to Sitges to end my day poolside. Maybe EJ was back and could entertain me.

Bored and restless on the train, I did the only thing I could do—text Jay.

What r u doin?

Finishing up work. What are you up to?

Went 2 erotic museeeem. Totes hotttt.

Oh boy. Shorthand and typos can only mean one thing haha How are you feeling over there?

Fuckin lonely. WTF. Why does Josh have a case?

LOL I don't know, Riss. Had a few drinks?

Dont judge me asshole. At least I dont lie to friends.

Whoa. Easy killer. What are you talking about?

Like u dont kno.

I don't. So why don't you tell me what's up.

Hows ur buddy bruce?

Uh, fine I guess. He's not a threat to your family, if that's what you're asking. I've been keeping an eye on everyone like I promised. What's the problem?

The problem is ur a liar. I kno about ur little date w him at the coffee shop.

How do u know about that?

Josh saw u so dont deny it. WTF Jay. I trusted u.

Riss, I have my reasons for meeting with him.

And?

I'm not getting into it with you like this. We'll talk later.

Sorry, no can do. Im done w u. have fun with ur new coffee buddy. byyyyeeeeeee

Whatever. Just be careful, Riss. Now that you have the statue in your possession, anyone could be lurking about. Watch your back, remember.

What the fuck? Is there a reason he used those specific words? And how in the hell did he know I had the statue already? Did I tell him? Fuck him, I'm not responding.

The room started to spin as I thought about how oddly ominous his words were. It wasn't like him to be so melodramatic; then again, I was text-bitching at him, so maybe he was just being defensive—or wanting to verbally slap me back in the face.

Still. I felt the goosebumps crawling up my back and down my arms. There was something unsettling about him and Bruce meeting, and now him not telling me why.

What if Josh was right? What if Jay had something to do with this, or was helping Bruce or someone else? Even Kevin had mentioned the possibility that someone on the outside could be trying to set the Marinos up. Could he possibly...

No, not Jay. He wouldn't hurt me or my family. Would

he? I mean, he had me slammed up against that wall and could have pummeled me if his body allowed him to do what his facial language wanted. Maybe I got out just in time before his psychopathic tendencies revealed themselves. You don't know a person until you live with them, they say.

I pulled up to the station and managed to get myself into a taxi and back to the villa before completely passing out. I might've had more sangria than I realized. It wasn't even four in the afternoon, but I fell onto my interim bed and didn't wake up until the middle of the night.

I missed a few calls and texts from Josh and some pleading texts from Jay to please respond that I was okay. I ignored the Jay texts but thought I would at least send Josh a quick apology text that I fell asleep early, loved him and would talk to him in the morning. I figured by now he'd definitely be asleep in bed. Not getting a response confirmed that.

A bit hungry, I made my way to the kitchen where I was relieved to find some leftover ham and cheese and a few crackers to nosh on. The house was eerily quiet—even the snores coming from EJ's room weren't loud enough to chase away the sound of solitude.

Ugh, I really hated being alone.

I tried falling back to sleep, but when that didn't work, I found myself in the studio. And there, in that space, was where I finally felt comfortable in my isolation. No one to walk in on me or ask questions about what I was working on. Perhaps this was solitary bliss after all.

I picked up the coveted paintbrush and went to work on my latest inspiration—thank you, Erotic Museum and endless sangria.

She was a gorgeous silhouette, laying there naked

on the canopy bed, her arms above her head in leather-bounded chains, her legs spread out in an exasperated 'V' and her chest turned slightly to the left.

A man knelt beside her by the bed, taking her one breast into his mouth, while he caressed the other with his fingers. In his other hand, he held a small whip raised in the air—ah, yes, and across her belly were the remnants of a red marking from the last strike.

His hardness was evident and on display, though untouched. He hungrily yearned for her, but he was not to be satiated; this painting and moment was all about her. Finally, about *her* and *only her.* And there was more.

There, at the base of her womanhood was the backside of a voluptuous blonde, the side of her face visible only enough to see her tongue reaching out towards her openness, her hands firmly keeping the silhouetted woman's legs in place.

Now with the scene set, I could more clearly define the receiving woman's carnal face, mouth gaping in rapture while a single tear from the pain-pleasure dichotomy fell from her closed eye.

Or, was it confusion over whether she wanted this kind of life anymore? Was it finally time for her to realize that sex was more than a game? Perhaps the tear beckoned her to relinquish the incessant need to feel worthy by giving her body to others for empty pleasure. Wishing the lash of each whip could slap out the feelings of shame left behind by a twisted high school teacher.

Where does the boundary between indulging in healthy fantasy and tawdry, scar-induced body abuse lie?

A question I'd face another time. My soul did not want to be bothered by such mental inquiries; it just wanted to feel. I wanted to express how okay it was to feel so satisfied with personal pleasure, right or wrong. How its escape is what I needed to get me through trying times, and I refused to apologize for it.

But all of the passion behind my painting, the memories and wounds they stirred up, were depleting my energy. Lost in exorcising what had been hidden within me for so long, I had no control over my own hands and heart to stop the flow of art or emotions.

I sat in the room painting for hours, not realizing how quickly time had passed until the sun peeked in from the window. Completely expelled of all creation, I decisively left my work of art to grab an orange juice and sit up on the rooftop to watch the sun rise over the glistening sea.

Now that I liberated the dark within, I could welcome in the beauty of the light.

The colors of red, orange and yellow ran together in a chaotic harmony as they fought their way to their proper place in the rising. Quiet, wondrous, peaceful.

I didn't resist the stillness.

Instead, I let my mind wander in this meditative moment to places that caught me off guard. Tears formed and forced their way out of their usually contained chocolate-colored cages.

I felt truly alone.

I didn't mean physically. I meant existentially.

I no longer knew who I could trust. Betrayal had been my only ally, alluring me into its web of suspicion. Jay was a lifelong friend, and yet his cryptic warnings and refusal to be straight with me made me question our 30-year history.

How about this new man of mine who promises me the world; the love of my life? Could I really believe that Josh could keep his jealousy in check—or better yet, honor his vow to love me exactly as I am and not abandon me like others had?

I questioned if my newly strengthened bond with my sisters would truly last beyond this trip. With all those unresolved hurts swirling around my heart, I feared that we would fall back into our individual lives once we hit American soil and I'd be the unimportant baby sister again.

Would Bruce completely win my mother over and take her away from us?

Would whoever sent that note come for me now that I had the statue?

Would I ever find true happiness? I never dared to allow myself to dream that I could ever have love, artistic success and a bright future. Am I deluding myself that just because I got a statue from an estranged grandfather that my life would actually change?

Questions—so many questions. And no answers.

Oh, hell no, brain. You're not going there. I'm not going to go talk to some bejeweled dragon. You're insane, I told myself.

Ignoring the curiosity within, I left the rooftop pool to brew a pot of coffee when I discovered EJ had already beat me to it. I was grateful for the company and the break in intense self-reflection.

"Well, good morning, sunshine! I don't ever think I've seen you up at the same time as the sun," he quipped a little too gleefully.

"I fell asleep early and then couldn't go back to bed. I've been working," I answered, trying to match his pep but failing.

"How wonderful! I hope it is more of that greatness you started with the dragon piece. I should like to see your work later," he remarked.

"Sure," I said nervously.

"Now tell me, what do you have planned for the day?"

"I don't know. I haven't thought that far ahead. I don't have the foggiest idea what to do with myself," I admitted.

"Well, how would you like to join me at the races today? Señor Dominguez down at the barber shop hooked me up with tickets to the Circuit de Catalunya racetrack in Montmeló, not too much more than an hour's trip away. I have an extra if you are interested?"

"Actually, that sounds perfect! What time's the train?"

"Oh, my dear, we are not going by train; we are going by bike. Meet me downstairs in two hours and we'll ride off in style."

The motorcycle EJ sat upon was stunning. A first class BMW® K 1600 GTL with an inline six-cylinder engine rumored to be smoother than silk on the road. Jay would absolutely die to get his ass on one of these babies.

Wiping the imaginary drool from my mouth, I walked up to the Godly machine and ran my hands along its steering. I was getting all warm and tingly inside just touching it.

"Should I leave you two alone and come back later?" EJ quipped.

"What? Oh," I reddened, realizing I had blocked him out to focus on this beauty. "Have you ever ridden something like this before?"

"Have I ever? Girl, I own one of these. Now, put on your helmet and hop on. We're about to go on the ride of a lifetime."

He wasn't kidding. This was no U.S. Highway thrill ride with a broody man. It was a fully immersive experience along the coast of the Mediterranean Sea. We practically drove up the edge of the beach as we made our way towards Barcelona, passing its many ports, marinas and even its own World Trade Center.

EJ was a natural rider, braving the curved roads with exhilaration and speed. I smartly wore my hair in a long braid, yet the escaped tendrils couldn't help but surrender to the gusts of wind.

Freedom. I could feel it once again, where there were no questions, no expectations, no conversations. Simply, freedom.

When all was said and done and this multi-country journey was over, I planned on buying my own freedom so that I could ride whenever I wanted to.

The raceway was packed with fans from across the nation and every kind of tourist you could imagine. We made it just in time for the opening ceremonies of the 24H Series, featuring both sports and touring car racing.

The crowds were lively, sporting the flags and colors representing their favorite driver. Cheers, hissing and chanting made the announcers almost inaudible, but it was hard not to fall into the spirit of the game. I had never been to a track before, and I was mesmerized by the adrenaline-pumping speed through the circuit and the edge-of-your-seat, near-miss crashes.

How terrifying and invigorating all at the same time. I made a mental note to look up nearby racetracks when I returned home; this was a spectator sport I could undeniably see myself getting into.

With many, many hours of racing left, EJ persuaded me to leave so we could enjoy some more of what Spain had to offer. I reluctantly agreed, not wanting to leave my newest addiction after a 6-hour viewing obsession. I was starting to get hungry, after all—for something more than a hot dog and alcohol-free beer.

We stopped at a small coastal town café, where we sat outside underneath a tiny umbrella with a magnificent view. As I stared out into the intoxicating water, I felt EJ watching me with a smirk.

"This is the first time I have seen you relax since the moment I met you, cuz. This suits you," he commented.

"I love riding. There is just something about it that liberates me from life."

"I can tell," he smiled. "I like this version of Marissa very much. It gives you balance."

"Balance?"

"Yes. We all need balance. I've witnessed your intensity in so many ways. This brings you to the opposite, more tranquil state of your being. Don't forget to nurture this side as well," he advised with a kind, caring tone before taking my hand and leading me back to the bike.

The rest of the way home was quiet, any sounds seized and carried away by the winds that hit our faces as we dared into the setting sun. Before long, we were back at the villa, refreshed and spent.

"Would it be all right if I came up and saw some of your paintings?"

"Okay. I—I'm not sure if I'm finished with them just yet."

"No, an artist's work is really never done. Even when completed, we always find something else that could've been done differently. We'd go on forever if we had the chance," he observed. "You don't need to be ashamed to show me. I already find you quite talented."

Begrudgingly, I escorted EJ to the studio where I unveiled my four paintings (including the completed blown glass one for Teresa).

"My, my," he spoke reverently, "How fast you work when inspired. And I don't mean as in rushed...I mean as in channeled, focused. Raw imagination versus planned perfection. I love them. Truly."

"Really?" His acclaim of my work meant the world to me as a fellow artist and renowned gallery owner.

"Yes. The use of colors isn't the captivator—it's the messages. How effortless and undiluted. I love how you reveal the sun's core to be less than perfect. And over here, what a marvelous expression of sexual decadence. They are daring, and I like that in an artist. I truly believe you have a vision, Marissa; one that needs to be seen."

"I don't know what to say. Thank you," I was speechless. Tears formed in my eyes.

"What's the matter, cuz?"

"Just—no one has ever expressed this much passion for or approval of my art. It's like for the first time, someone sees me and acknowledges me. It feels—unreal."

"Come, cuz. Let's go grab some cava and talk out on the balcony. I think there is much more to say," he said gently. Usually I would put my defenses up, sensing a lecture, but with EJ, we had this kindred connection that made me feel safe and unjudged.

Settled down deep into the cushioned chairs with glasses of the ticklish bubbly, we took in the view before breaking the silence with what was sure to be a heavy conversation. But I think I was ready for it.

"Where to begin?" he pondered. "Tell me, what were the motivations behind your recent paintings? It's more than just an impulse—there is history there. Talk to me—artist to artist, blood to blood."

"Okay," I started, not sure what to tackle first. "So, the dragon blackening the heart—I kinda told you that I was fighting with both my boyfriend and best friend."

"Yes, I remember. Go on," he encouraged.

"Well, there was more to it," I confessed. And then, after so many years, I was able to share my story to an open ear who was both sympathetic and respectful of my privacy. He said not a word but held my hand as I bravely recounted the memory that pushed me to create.

"In that moment, when the brush touched the canvas, I felt like love was impossible. That it wasn't all sonnets and flowers, and as much as I wanted to love and give of my whole heart, there was always this darkness that betrayed it. Lies, abandonment, lack of trust. That my heart, or any heart I tried to love, was not pure like they claim love is. That there is always something waiting in the shadows to darken it."

"And yet, there is still hope."

"Yes, exactly. I guess it's just my way of wrapping my head around the fact that love's not perfect, but it's still worth it. That the dragon, so to speak, can come for it, but it cannot—will not—have it all. That the heart's resiliency can win out after all."

"I can see how this mirrors your teenage experience, and I am so sorry you had to face that alone. But I also have to ask—does this reflect your current love life as well?"

"It does. I love Josh with all of my heart. He's the one; I know it. He is handsome and understanding and him having money doesn't hurt, either," I admitted. "He's been so supportive throughout this entire year, ever since we found out about this secret grandfather."

"And how does he feel about you?"

"He says he loves me, and I believe that. I think." I saw EJ raise an eyebrow. "Well, I'm slow to believe any man could love me, because no one has ever done so before. So, I am treading lightly."

"Treading lightly, or blocking intuition?"

"What do you mean?"

"There is a very thin line between fear because you are trying to protect yourself and fear because it's a warning signal. What keeps you so guarded?"

"I'm not certain."

"He is the first man you think ever loved you, you say?"

"I know he is."

"Hmm. And don't get angry for this question, it's just a question—are you finding yourself more drawn to the idea of love, or to Josh himself? I ask because sometimes when we get a glimmer of what we have always so desperately wanted, we cling on to it for dear life and never see the red flags."

"I mean, no one is perfect, right? We do have some differences, but I'd like to think we are working on them and that our love is real."

"That's not what I asked," he gently delved. "You don't need to give me an answer, dear heart. But you do need to ask and answer it yourself," he added. "Now, how about this Jay fellow? What about him and your relationship?"

"We're just friends. I've known him since we were kids."

"Okay, but you were also angry with him. Why?"

"He lied to me. Well, not that he lied, but he withheld something important from me, and when I confronted him, he wasn't forthcoming."

"I see. And how did that make you feel?"

"You know, for an artist, you certainly would make a great therapist," I remarked, as he laughed.

"Why, thank you. I'll consider that for my next life. Now, continue. Unless you would be more comfortable on the couch?" I loved how this crazy cousin of mine matched my sarcastic wit. I realized then that I was so glad he lived close enough to visit on occasion. Absolutely hands down, my favorite person, probably on this entire planet.

"Fine," I laughed with him. "I have known him my whole life, and we never kept secrets from each other. And now, it feels like he is. Ever since our big fight and he moved out, he has been distant and unreadable. Like I don't know who he is anymore."

"Ah, well that happens sometimes in life. But now I can see where the dragon painting came in. Your fears, anger, sense of betrayal, confusion, yet wanting to hold on. Thank you for sharing all that."

"You're welcome. I actually feel like a weight was lifted off me, getting it all out in the open. Thank you for listening."

"Of course. But we're not done yet," he smirked. "The torn sun picture."

"So, with that one, I had some really disturbing nightmares—which are happening more and more frequently while I am here, by the way." I shuddered at the thought of the blood-dripping scaly monsters chasing after me and images of loved ones turning into demons with black hearts.

"You know, dreams and nightmares are messages that our subconscious is trying to send to us. There is powerful symbolism that if captured, can unlock your own mysteries."

"Well, if that is the case, then I have pretty twisted insides," I lamented.

"Take notice of who is in them, what is happening around you and how it resolves—if at all. You may get a pattern. Just something to think about offline," he suggested.

"Okay, I will. So, the torn sun. Oh boy, if I am being honest—" I had to pause and take a deep breath.

"That was me, tearing apart my perfect sisters to show they are not really all that perfect. I am tired of living in their shadows when they have plenty of their own. I'm not the only one with darkness and I wanted to expose them as frauds." Silence. "Oh my God, I can't believe I said that out loud."

"Honey, I told you, I would never judge, and I am not. My lack of response was allowing you to absorb the enormity of what you just said for yourself. You are the one judging, sweetie."

"So, you don't think I am completely depraved for thinking this?"

"Not at all. When people do not understand each other, and it's not communicated, it can sometimes fester into this heightened sense of bitterness. I know you love your sisters and would never hurt them. If I thought that, I'd have you committed," he joked, though I'm pretty sure he meant it.

"But the problem is, I had just had a wonderful conversation with both of them to clear up all of our repressed feelings. I felt our bond restored. I'm not sure why I still felt compelled to create this."

"Conversations are healing; but even after the words are said and apologies accepted, remnants remain that need to be worked out and healed. The scars still need to be addressed so that you can become whole again. Tell me, after painting that, did you feel more at ease with them?"

"Come to think of it, I did," I was floored to admit that.

"Wonderful, then well done. I won't tell them they are the subjects," he teased. "And now for this exquisite *ménage à trois?"*

"Yeah, about that one. Um, I'm not sure I want to talk about it."

"Girlfriend, I'm an openly homosexual man and I ain't got anything against the kinky. Spill it."

Nervously chuckling, I relented. Why the hell not? He was learning everything else about me.

"I have always been the black sheep of the family— you know, the one drawn to experiment with drugs and sex, and I even have this obsessive attraction to crime. Not committing them, but watching those suspense shows and hearing about real life stories. I want to know what makes those animals tick and how clever they must be to get away with that shit.

"Maybe that's why out of the three of us, I'm the least freaked out by all of the drama following us. It enthralls me to be a part of something like that.

"Anyway, I'm what someone politically correct would call sexually fluid. I love men first and foremost. But I also love the touch and scent of a woman every now and then. I love multiple lovers at once, and some light bondage and—I don't know, a little bit of pain heightens the pleasure for me."

I looked down, beet red, utterly embarrassed that I was exposing all of this to a 50-something-year-old gay man I just met a month ago.

"It's all right," EJ assured me. "I'm listening. Why do you think it appeals to you so?"

"I—I think it's freedom. I don't like to be told what to do or be limited by society, so I think I act out against it. It also, well, keeps me safe from commitment. Josh enjoys it and indulges me—but as I watch him with another woman and I'm with another man, I wonder if it's the safe zone that lets us love without obligation. Or, that I let myself be used in this way to hold on to what I am so afraid to lose, when what I should really be afraid of is losing myself.

"Holy crap. I never thought of it that way," I surprised myself with my own insight. "I wondered why her tear felt so powerful to me. Now I see it tells a bigger story than I even imagined."

"Well, my sweet cousin, seems to me you have uncovered a lot and have some feelings to sort through," he said, rising up from his chair to give me a kiss on the forehead. "Might I suggest that conversation with your dragon statue now, and a day at the beach tomorrow to ponder it all?"

"You really think me talking to that thing will help?"

"I do. There are some things that, even as open as you were with me, you held back from. The dragon for certain will not spill your secrets—and someone should listen if only to let you hear them for yourself. Ask yourself what it is you truly want in life, Marissa. Let the answers come to you like they did tonight."

"I'll think about it," I obliged, as he smiled warmly and wished me good night.

I couldn't yet bring myself to talk to some onyx stone, and even with questions driving down the roadways of my brain, I needed to check in with Josh before I fell asleep. I missed him and just wanted to hear his voice.

"What's that noise?"

"Oh, just the courtroom. Lots of people here today. Been a hectic day."

"At this time of night?"

"Yeah, um, big murder trial going on. Lots of press. Listen, Mar, I gotta go. I just wanted to pick up and hear your voice."

"Only three more days," I pointed out.

"I know. I can't wait to see you, babe. I've missed you so much and have hated all this fighting."

"Me too."

"Hey, I've been meaning to ask you—did you get your statue yet?"

"Oh, I thought I told you. Sorry. I did. It's beyond incredible, Josh. It's a double-headed onyx dragon laced with rare stones and crystals. Wait until you see it."

"Soon, my love. Soon, you will be in my arms and you can tell me everything."

Deciding to ignore my cousin's advice for one more day, I chose to let myself fall into a deep sleep instead of chat with an ancestral heirloom. There was always tomorrow for that one.

10

I spent a great deal of time looking at my reflection in the mirror the next morning. At times, I knew exactly who Marissa Rossi was. At other times, the girl looking back at me was just a stranger.

The question replayed over and over in my mind like a skipping record. *What do I want in life?*

It would haunt me for most of the day.

I did take EJ's advice to go to the beach—but not just any beach. With my sisters and their rather prude outlook on life (at least publicly), I couldn't exactly suggest that we experience the nude beach together, so I was going to jump on the opportunity to check one out while they were gallivanting through France.

Grabbing my suntan oil, a light lunch, my phone and my headphones, I headed out to Sitges' local Playa de las Balmins.

Being midweek with school in session and summer winding down, it wasn't especially crowded. Though predominantly gay, it was welcoming to all walks of life—surprisingly, even to families with young children. Not everyone chose to strip down, but those that did must not have had a care in the world.

They certainly weren't the buff, hot volleyball players I expected, that's for sure.

But I was game, sinking down into the sand and

removing every last article of clothing that restricted me. I made sure, however, to put extra sunscreen on my most sensitive areas—a burn there must be excruciatingly painful.

Turning on my tunes to the welcome alternative rock sounds of Foals, I soaked up the sun, feeling the warmth penetrate my cells and create that glistening moisture of sweat all over.

After a while, I sat up to enjoy people watching while grabbing a snack. Couples were rubbing lotion on each other's backs. Kids were playing tag with the waves that crashed onto the sand, trying to pull them in. Girlfriends were gossiping in Spanish with drinks in hand under their shady umbrellas.

Everyone seemed so—content.

And I did, too; temporarily.

What would make me this blissfully happy all the time? Would it be to marry Josh? Maybe I could buy a house. Own an art gallery. Get a motorcycle. All of the above? What *did* I want?

I tried to make a mental checklist of the things I thought would make me happy, but at the end of the day, they all seemed empty. I was missing something but couldn't put my finger on it. Not wanting to get lost in my over-analyzing and burn to a crisp, I packed up my things and headed back to the villa.

I laid there on my bed, still confused as to the purpose of my life. It prompted me to text my mom, sisters, Josh, Jay and even some random friends just so I would not have to feel this sense of loneliness amid the deep white comforter.

Of course, most everyone was busy, some not even texting back. Mom and Granny were out at an end-of-summer day fair while the kids were at camp. Meg and Mia were sending pictures of themselves in berets eating crepes at a cute little outdoor café. They looked like they were having the time of their lives—together. Without me.

Josh quickly replied that he was still in court. Jay never responded (probably working or on his bike). My best girl friend, Jenna, was getting ready to go on a hike and another friend, Em, was getting her nails done. Even EJ wasn't around, off enjoying some more sights—though, of course, his response was a prompt to remember what we had talked about.

Ugh, as if I could forget our heavy conversation last night. I've been trying all day to block it from my brain.

My confusion over whether I was just settling for Josh because someone finally loved me. Or, if I was being too quick to judge Jay's trustworthiness just because he didn't tell me the whole story yet. Why on earth did EJ have to plant those contemplations in my head, like I don't question my life enough?

I thought about how I lived in the shadows of my sisters, noticing how different and how drawn to the "bad things" in life I was. How I kept comparing myself to them and never measuring up.

I remembered EJ's observation, and my own revelation, that I needed to find that equilibrium between intensity and peace. Staring at the exquisite double-headed dragon on my dresser, it occurred to me that it represented balance.

Balance. That's what my life was missing. Either I was independent or co-dependent. A workaholic or a bum. Successful or caught in the daily grind. Accepted or outcast. Black sheep or proud daughter.

It's how I've always been, though. But he was right—I had to find a way to bring all these parts of me together. I erred on the side of passion; whatever could give me a thrill. I was ignoring the softer parts of me to protect myself from being hurt again.

I picked up the statue and gazed at its two sides. Light and dark. Both parts of one body. A united front. Him and her, as the antique shop owner had said. Yin and yang. Life. *My* life.

Holy crap, was this really the answer to everything?

My epiphanies took off like a race car on the Circuit de Catalunya racetrack.

Through reckless riding, drugs or even push-it-to-the-limit sex, I was numbing the part of me that craved security and love. If I put myself in the danger, then I was in control. I would be the one to hurt me—not anyone else. It was a choice I made a long time ago when I thought I couldn't live up to family expectations; when I believed Mr. Terrance's assessment that I was nothing more than a body to use. Might as well give the world what it thinks I am.

But I am more than that, I asserted, fighting back a few tears. I am just as intelligent as Meg and just as kind as Mia. I am much more than a pretty face. I have the drive to make my dreams come true and a heart that deserves true love. Real, genuine love.

Even with Josh, I knew I was still guarded. I used sexual fantasies to keep him lured in; content, aroused and entertained enough so that he wouldn't want to leave me.

But what if I didn't indulge? What if I removed the mask and let vulnerability shine through?

Sure, I enjoyed a kink every now and then. But

what surprised me was how powerfully affected I was that night Josh and I actually made pure love, without the extravaganza. How he moved within me slowly, deeply, connecting with me—rather than enjoying some fantastical game.

That night together sparked something within me I hadn't known was there. A desire for affection and gentleness over rushed and rowdy. A completeness. I wanted more of that kind of love, that kind of touch, that kind of deep bond. I yearned for it.

I want to be more than just this temple of pleasure. To find more depth in life than to escape into moans and orgasms. To find a balance between sexual expression and meaningful intimacy. That is what I wanted—no, that is what I *needed.*

Would Josh be open to shifting our sex life to be more intimate like that night? Or would he run for the hills? Bigger question: am I brave enough to find out?

My reflections then shifted over to my paintings— another soul awakening revelation. I didn't have to paint the pretty; I didn't have to produce something just for others' approval. I desired to reach people's innermost repressed feelings to give them permission to embrace their murkier stirrings without guilt.

Honoring our forbidden notions doesn't make any of us "bad" people. We all have a bit of anger that darkens our hearts when love burns us; but it doesn't turn our heart to complete black. We can heal from it.

We all have that contrasted core of brightness and obscurity, and it shouldn't take someone ripping at us to accept that we are still whole, with both sides a strong part of us. We can shine and depress like the ebb and flow of the ocean. It's an innate part of our human psyche to rise and fall.

And we all have those sexual fantasies—perhaps not exactly as depicted in my painting, with multiple sexual partners or erotic pain—but we do all have that desire to receive pleasure in the way that arouses us without shame. Whatever those fantasies are for us as individuals are perfectly natural.

Interesting—it is in my art that I can see my own balance. Just like this two-headed dragon. Both sides of me can come together and be expressed. Though I do feel compelled to finally add more illumination to even it out, the dark does not need to "win." It just needs to be seen and acknowledged and loved just as much as the light.

It's not supposed to be a fight; it's a mutual compromise. Not one or the other. Both.

And it all starts within me. I can be a more vulnerable person if I accept that love can sometimes hurt but never destroy—unless I let it. It may or may not work out with Josh, or in my friendships, or even with my family. But to have that feeling of being loved is worth the risk, more than protecting myself and shutting out the potential.

I can be a better sister by not judging Meg or Mia for what I deem to be their worst sides, and not projecting my jealousy onto them when they shine. I just need to honor my own capacity for the spotlight and strive for it, knowing I am imperfect and so are they. I can transcend this pettiness and embrace the love that they offer me and give it right back to them.

I don't need to use my body in exchange for love and attention. I can enjoy sexual carnalities that truly entice me, but not the constant theatrics I feel are necessary to keep someone interested. That is not love; that is desperation to fill a hole in my heart.

I am *not* a broken young girl any longer.

I want to receive pleasure that is given freely and without condition. Josh could be that man, but it was a test I would have to give him. We had to be more than outstanding sex. I deserved the whole package.

Wow. If Meg were here, she'd say something about how these trips really bring out my "uncharacteristically deep" thoughts. It's a comment I would've usually gotten mad at. But now I'm saying the same words to myself, recognizing that my thoughts are more golden than I give them credit for.

That's when it hit me. I knew exactly what I wanted in life. Like I said to Josh, I wanted respect. I wanted respect, acceptance *and* love.

But I had to give those to myself first before expecting others to give them to me.

I let the awakening wash over me in the shower as I inhaled the lavender scents of my shampoo. The cleansing bubbles and warm water washed away the world that was holding me back; releasing me from the cage I put myself in.

I felt refreshed and vibrant; alive with new purpose and a determination to make the best out of life. I had conquered my demons by embracing them, and by finally allowing myself to be reflected in my art. I now get how crucial this time alone was for me—for each of us on our respective journeys. It gave me a whole new perspective on my sisters and their individual battles, and their wins. I couldn't wait for them to come home tomorrow so I could share all that I learned.

Oh, how I wished EJ was in the house so I could tell

him about my powerful revelations—and then maybe he would divulge the mystery of the dragon to me!

The wait would be torture, but there was one thing I could do while I waited for everyone: I could try to find that hidden map. I turned the sculpture every which way to see if I could find an inkling of an opening. Not under the base, not in the flames—though I did find the two tongues to be quite loose. I'd have to see someone about getting those tightened up.

Where could it be, damn it? I thought I might have stumbled upon the secret when I saw an envelope sticking out of my purse by the door.

Strange—has it been here this whole time?

Reading it, I could feel the color drain from my face. On instinct, I dialed Jay's number. Straight to voicemail. I tried calling his work but they said he had abruptly taken a few days off for a family emergency. I called his mom, but there was no answer there, either.

Where the fuck was he?

Ready or not, here I come. For what is rightfully mine.

I looked at the note again. Same font as the last one. But how on earth did it get into my purse? Did someone slip it in there while I was at the beach?

The thought of some creep sneaking up on me as I laid naked on the sand sent chills down my spine. I felt violated, like I needed to take another shower to wash away the disgust I was feeling.

Come on, Jay, I begged as it went to voicemail yet again. I began to panic. I didn't know what to do. Should I tell Meg and Mia? Should I call EJ? Should I tell the guards, or call Kevin?

I regretted my previous decision to follow jealous impulses instead of protecting my family; this time, I wasn't going to keep the note a secret. But first, I had to get ahold of someone—anyone at this point!

I had to clear my head. I needed to go for a walk so I could figure out my next steps. I planned to alert one of the guards that I needed surveillance, and would instruct the other to safeguard the house.

I left a message with the note on the kitchen table for EJ to find, so that he knew what was going on and could stay safe until I returned. I let him know I was with one of the guards and that I would be back soon—to call me if anything else happened.

Before I could make my way out, there was a knock at the door. Petrified and no longer enjoying being in a suspense thriller, I carefully peeked out of the bedroom window to see who it was first.

Josh!

"Oh my God, I am so glad to see you," I cried, rushing into his arms and squishing the beautiful bouquet of lilies he had in his hands.

"Marissa, what's wrong?" He pulled me away from him with concern, wiping my tears with his fingers.

"I—I got another note. Someone is still out there, Josh. Someone is still trying to hurt us," I spit out, rushing right back into the safety of his arms. He gently moved us so that we were inside the lobby and closed the door.

"What are you talking about, babe? I can barely understand you," he said, guiding me to the bright blue armchair before I passed out from panic.

I finally admitted to him about the first note, begging for forgiveness for not telling him or anyone else sooner—and how I was afraid he would be so overprotective that I would never get to come here and get my heirloom. I told him about my interaction with Bruce, them rambled about how selfish I was, and how I have now put everyone I love in danger—in between gushing repetitions of relief over seeing him.

"Does anyone know about these notes?"

"I told my sisters a few days ago." Then with a guilty look, I whispered, "And Jay."

"You told *him* but not me?" His fury began to rise, but quickly dissipated as he saw me in such angst over it.

"I knew he couldn't stop me from going. Plus, he was level-headed enough to keep an eye on Bruce for me. But I can't get ahold of him."

"I might know why. This explains a lot, Marissa. I wish you had told me sooner."

"Explains what?"

"Jay and Bruce meeting. Me not being able to find Jay the last two days. I had a suspicion something was off, so I did some investigating. I don't know how to say this, but I found out something unsettling about your best friend. One of his closest pals from college was Thomas Marino—Peggy and Patrick's son."

"What? That's not possible," I said in disbelief. "He would never—I've known him forever, Josh."

"I know. I'm so sorry, sweetheart. But as soon as I found that out, I needed to get here to you. Since no one can reach him, I can only assume he has made his way to Spain. Turns out my instincts could be right—I need to protect you myself. And I want no arguing this time," he insisted.

Stunned and heartbroken, I nodded my head and awaited his direction. He immediately was on the phone booking a private cottage for us; somewhere Jay couldn't find us until everyone came back tomorrow. I forgot to tell him about the message I left for EJ, but we didn't have time for me to revise it with further details. I'd just call to check in later.

Grabbing just enough for an overnight bag, I moved in a daze as he barked orders at me to hurry. So much to process. How had I never known Jay was best friends with a Marino? How naïve could I be?

"Mar, we have to get going before anyone finds us. Do you have the dragon?" I nodded.

"Good. Let's go," he rushed, stopping briefly to convince the guards that we were in no danger and that he would keep an eye out for me. They looked at me for confirmation, and I nodded and smiled, asking them to please watch over the house and I'd be back later.

It was seamless, rehearsed and believable, just as we had conned the guards before when we were in Ireland and Italy to have some alone time together. We had this scheme down to a science.

About fifteen minutes later, we arrived at a quaint little cottage somewhere in between Sitges and Barcelona. Nestled into what appeared to be a national park, there was nothing and no one around except hiking trails, a stunning view and perhaps a few wildlife.

"We'll be safe here tonight," he assured me. He wrapped his strong arms around my back and held me as I broke down in sobs. He stood quiet, letting me emote and ramble and slobber all over his cashmere sweater without flinching.

He brought me over to the queen-sized bed and sat me down, removing the wet strands of hair from my face and lifting up my chin.

"Promise me you will never keep anything like this

from me again," he pleaded.

"I promise. I am so sorry," I replied.

"If anything were to ever happen to you…" he broke off mid-sentence, choking back his own sobs that threatened to take over.

"I love you," was all I could muster up. I looked at him with my tear-stained face, and he brought me in for a passionate kiss. He instantly had me on my back, tearing off my clothes with the hunger of a man who had not eaten in weeks.

But I had to stop him. I didn't want savagery right now. I needed his pure love and protection.

"Please, can we be gentle tonight?" I implored. He smiled and obliged, slowing down his passionate fury to kiss me more delicately. Not as much tender foreplay as I was hoping for, as his hands still anxiously went straight for my swelled opening.

My phone rang—I stopped him enough to see that it was Mia. He groaned in agony.

"Please, Marissa, I've missed you. You can call her back after we make love. I need you," he groveled as he continued to play with my breasts and finger my insides. I conceded, turning my ringer to silent and letting him devour me with as much patience as the man could find to somewhat honor my request for slow and steady. I needed him as much as he needed me.

His tongue traveled from inside my ear, down the curve of my breasts, over my tightened stomach and down into me. He squeezed my ass as he impeccably flicked his tongue against my clit, causing the heat to rise within me. Sensing my pre-orgasm arch, he stopped to move his kisses up to my mouth so that he could slide inside me instead.

Rhythmic throbs as his drenched body rubbed up against mine, the fire between us burning even hotter. He kissed me like there was no tomorrow, before swiftly moving his mouth to take a hard bite of my nipple, making me scream as his final plunge nailed me hard. He knew all too well that this would make me explode simultaneously.

Part of me loved when he did that, so that we released together. But I didn't want that tonight. I freed the disappointment from my mind, as I felt him pull me into a spooning caress, stroking my hair with deep affection and placing a kiss on top of my head. I could hear his heartbeat, and before I knew it, I was sound asleep in his arms.

His hardened cock woke me in the middle of the night, finding its way into me for another round. Groggy, I didn't put up a fight, and just let him pleasure himself without bringing me to orgasm. I'd save the conversation about a new way of lovemaking for another time. I didn't want to fight; I just wanted to remain safe and protected here in his arms.

In the morning, I found him standing over the bed, naked but holding a tray of blackened coffee and a pastry, complemented by a small white vase with a single red rose.

"Good morning, beautiful," he said cheerfully.

"Good morning," I cooed back. "What's all this?"

"I figured you could use some sustenance. We have a few hours before I take you back and I thought we should take advantage of this private time," he suggested.

"Thank you. I'm starving," I replied as I bit into the flaky croissant with decadent chocolate inside.

"Hey, where's that statue by the way? I'd love to see it."

"Oh, of course. It's over here in my bag," I said as I went to retrieve it and carefully remove it from its protective wrapping. There it was—I could look at it a million times and still be in awe of it.

"It's as splendid as you claimed it was," said Josh in matching awe. "May I?"

He took it into his hands and ran his fingers over it with the same softness I did, taking in every inch of its rich features.

"What have you learned about it?"

"Not much," I admitted. "Its composition is black onyx with a marble base, and it has ruby and sapphire eyes and red opal and citrine flames. Goya is confirmed as its creator, one of his very first pieces. EJ hasn't told me yet what it represents, but I think I figured it out. One head represents good, the other evil, but they are made from one body and part of each other. Just like I am."

He looked over and smiled at me. "Though I must say, I like your evil side a little better," he joked. I bashfully grinned, not knowing if I should take that as a compliment. I heard EJ's voice of warning. Red flags were popping up; I was starting to get the feeling that as much as he supported me, the sex was more important to him. But I'd save that investigation for another time, when we were safe back in the states.

"Oh, I almost forgot. There is also a map hidden within the statue. It's a guide to the keys that open the jewelry box, where EJ said there is a greater inheritance awaiting us."

"Is that so?"

"Yes. Once everyone arrives for the party—and we find the map—we will learn how to open it all together as a family."

"Interesting. But you haven't found the map yet?"

"Not exactly, but before I got that horrible note last night, I think I stumbled upon a crack in the tail…perhaps if I twist it, it will open."

"Clever girl," he said slyly, making his way over to the bed, trailing kisses down my neck and removing the coffee cup from my hand. His tongue thrust into my mouth, pulling me into a heightened arousal that made me want him to touch me endlessly.

He stepped back with a smirk, reaching into the drawer beside me and pulling out four sets of handcuffs and bonds.

"We played it your way last night. Indulge me, would you?" he asked so sweetly, yet seductively. I acquiesced by raising my arms above my head so he could strap each one to the bedpost, and then spread my legs apart so he could tie them up as well.

He took an ice cube from the bucket and ran it down the length of my body, concentrating it around my nipples to create stinging sensations before biting them hard.

"Ow, Josh, you're hurting me," I whimpered. "Take it easy."

He ignored my pleas, biting harder and moving the ice cube all the way down and into me. The sensation was at first unbearable, but as it melted with my heat, the pain eased. He then taunted me with the sight of another ice cube, clearly wanting a repeat performance.

"Josh, stop it. Please." Throwing the block to the floor, he angrily straddled me until his face was only an inch away from mine.

"I'll do whatever I damn well please to you, bitch. You're mine, and if I want to stick ice cubes up your pussy, I will. Lucky for you, I'd much rather fuck you hard and senseless. You should have watched your back like I warned you to. Stupid whore."

The evil smile spread over his face and his maniacal laugh sent chills colder than the ice throughout my body.

Joshua Perkins was the mastermind all along.

11

Mercilessly, he didn't come near me—yet. Instead, he seemed disgusted at the sight of me.

"What's wrong, Marissa? Perk up, you kinky slut. You're no fun to fuck when you're lifeless."

"Why are you doing this?" I furiously hissed, traumatized enough not to cry but embarrassed enough to realize I was locked up and spread eagle, unable to move or get away from this psychopath if he chose to touch me.

"Because I can," he spat. "Because finally, I am the one in control. I knew you would be my ticket," he sneered, dancing around like a crazy Christmas elf.

"All I needed to do was make you believe I loved you, and you'd spill your guts to me. Fuck, you were so predictable. Oh, and it was a bonus that you happened to be into all this bondage and orgy shit. Had you not gone sensitive and wanted 'gentle lovemaking,' I might have even put up with you for a while longer.

"But now you're making my dick soft," he grumbled in disapproval, playing with himself to try to get erect again.

"So, you've been lying this whole time?" I asked incredulously. How could I have been so blind? What was wrong with my internal warning system that I didn't see this coming?

"Yes, sweetheart. How else could I get close to your

sainted family? I knew prissy Meg would be too smart and catch on, and well, I wasn't really into the roly-poly married one with the cop up her ass. You were dumb and desperate, so I went for the baby of the family and hit the jackpot."

"I don't understand why?"

"Why, princess? Because that's *my* fucking fortune. MINE," he spewed in intense anger.

"I'm sorry, how is this yours?" I was beginning to feel the fight rise back up in me. This man that I thought I loved lied to me, betrayed me and possibly intended to rape me—or worse. No way was I backing down now. If he was going to violate me, I was going to get some answers first.

"That's none of your business, bitch. All you need to know is that this little gem is stolen property, and I intend to claim it back. All of it." He grabbed the dragon statue and kissed it, hugging it to his chest as he laughed in sinister relief.

"You won't get away with this, asshole. Someone will find me, and you'll go down."

"Like who? Like your sisters who don't care about you? Some fag who is off at a nude beach getting his jollies? Some biker dude you cut off because I persuaded you that he betrayed you? The guards we slipped by? I don't think so, sweetheart. No one knows where you are. I'll be long gone by the time anyone finds your rotting corpse."

"You wouldn't dare."

Now fully dressed in his clothes, he walked up to me and stuck his face in mine again, practically spitting on me with his hateful vengeance. "Watch me."

Oh my God, he meant it. I saw it in his possessed,

raging eyes. He was going to kill me.

Way to go, Marissa. You've finally gotten yourself into a mess you can't get out of. All because of your selfish desires for a dragon statue, a fortune and all the joy money promised you.

Against my better judgment, I began to cry.

"Oh, knock it off, you baby," he said as he slapped me across the face. As I recuperated from the sting, I felt the slightest hint of blood drip down from the corner of my mouth.

"Maybe baby wants to hear a little bedtime story before she goes bye-bye?" he chided with a cold, childish mock. "Want to know how I did it?"

I looked defiantly at him, trying to find whatever dignity I could muster. If these were my last moments on earth, I'd go down demons blazing.

"I'll take that as a yes?" He strolled over to the red high back armchair in the corner of the room and crossed his legs, a smug look of satisfaction upon his face as he played with a box of matches he picked up from the nearby table.

"Once upon a time there was a hypocritical old man who betrayed his family, first by lying about his bastard child and then by leaving a fortune to a bunch of lower-class nobodies.

"One by one, his adopted and blood family members received grand gestures—houses, riches, estates—while the one grandson who was there for him, who served him until his dying day, got a damn Rolex watch and a pat on the back. The least the fucker could have done was reinstate me to the family," he said, breaking from his singsong storytelling to expose the secret behind his wrath.

"Reinstate you?"

"Yeah, sweetheart. I was born Joshua Marino, youngest son of David and Bethany, brother to sainted Patrick and Colin. But I never measured up to the prides and joy of the family, and one wrong move landed me in jail.

"Tarnished the family name they said, so they excused me from it, as luck would have it," he said bitterly, reliving his personal nightmare.

"Then how did you end up as my grandfather's lawyer? If everyone knew you to be the rotten son of a bitch you clearly are, then why would he bother with you?"

I relished in the opportunity to pour the salt into his wound. *Maybe I shouldn't instigate him,* I thought to myself, *but what did I have to lose at this point?* It seemed the more I angered him, the more he wanted to reveal. And I wanted to know every last detail.

"The dumbasses underestimated me. When they were all at a little family party—one where they seemed to have lost my invitation—I broke into good old Grandpa's study and found a damaging tell-all journal and an old photo of him with a sexy little minx and a bratty kid, the words 'Lillith and Alissa' scribbled on the back of it.

"I confronted him about it, bringing him to his knees. All I had to do was threaten to expose him or hurt them, and he was putty in my hands."

"You blackmailed him."

"If you want to call it that, then technically, yes. I saw it as finding my way back to my family's loving arms," he said in defense of his actions.

"I asked to be made a Marino again, but he said the rest of the family would never accept it; it would be too much and they'd never go along with it. Pissed and weak,

I compromised and agreed to take Perkins as my last name, be dubbed his lawyer and receive a piece of the inheritance when he croaked.

"The family was resistant to his decision to name me as his lawyer, but as the patriarch, they believed his claims of wanting to keep the family intact due to honor or some shit. Whatever, they bought it. I tried to push repeatedly to be let back in, but he got the upper hand when he softened and came clean about his bastard family to everyone. Sentimental asshole," he spat.

"I was irate. I had nothing left to hold over his head, with them being all forgiving and shit. He met enough stipulations that would satisfy the wishes of dead Uncle Rocco, so they allowed him to remain as head of the family.

"He lost nothing. He betrayed his word and the ancestral wishes, and he lost NOTHING. Yet, I couldn't be forgiven for one little accidental murder in my teens," he muttered bitterly.

"I guess I should be grateful to the geezer that he never ratted me out to the family for 'blackmailing him,' as you called it. I confronted him about it and he said that I was in enough trouble with the family and he wanted to leave it all behind us. Too much family disruption as it was, the pussy said.

"Anyway, to keep peace, he kept me on as his lawyer and made me jump through hoops to prove myself as worthy of staying that way. It was complete torture. I had to pretend my ass off that I was rehabilitated and trustworthy—no small feat, but that practice certainly came in handy with you, princess," he leered with self-gratification.

"Of course, after all that hard work, he still stiffed me

in the end and left me nothing. Nothing but instructions to carry out a plan he had for his 'dear Lillith' and 'little diamond' and gag me with the rest."

"But you weren't even mentioned in the will," I pointed out.

"Yes, I was. Are you even paying attention? I got a Rolex watch. One goddamn watch," he yelled irritably. "But since you are so stupid, I guess I should remind you that I'm the one who read the will to you. I conveniently left out reading my name so you didn't catch on. I counted on you never reading the will in detail after that, which was something else that worked in my favor. You were all so emotional about Grampy's farewell letters that you missed what was right in front of your face."

"And so now you think that because of all this, you are entitled to our heirlooms?"

"Yes, damn it, I am. My father was the one raised by him and took his name. Not your slut Mahoney, Rossi, whatever of a mother. My brothers got their share from the Marino side. It would only be fair for me to receive equivalent value, so I thought instead of fighting my brothers and worsening the family feud, I could hoodwink great-grandmother Lena's side and make a killing for myself." He was so damn proud of himself and his smug treachery. If I could kick him in the nuts…

"'These letters are not to be opened by anyone except the Rossi family,' he warned me. Like the good little puppy dog I was, I promised him with every repentant cell in my body that I would honor his final wishes. Ha! The fool.

"Like I wouldn't steam open the envelopes, read the letters and then reseal them before delivering them to you. Like your old bat of a grandmother would remember

Leigh's real handwriting versus my forged one on new 'sealed' envelopes."

"You're such a creep," I couldn't help but comment.

"Yeah, but a smart one. My plan was brilliant—and clearly, it worked. The moment I met you, I knew I would get everything I wanted. It was so easy to penetrate you—literally and figuratively," he laughed, rising from the chair to run a finger down my body and tweak my nipple.

He stood there and toyed with the idea of touching me more as he continued his diabolical monologue. I cringed at the feeling of his finger circling my stomach and suggestively moving lower.

"You were so desperate to be wanted that you went along with all my ideas, believing my lies about needing information every step of the way to protect you. You sang like a canary, sweetheart. Where everybody was, about the decoys, about the warnings and about your plans for security. You made it so fucking easy, doll face.

"It makes me almost sad to kill you when I should be so grateful," he taunted as his breath drew to a whisper near my earlobe, taking a prolonged nibble and licking my neck. Thankfully, he was too engrossed in his own story to continue his sexual torment.

"I worried about you catching on all those times when the break-ins and notes happened, but then you so innocently believed my whereabouts every single time. Didn't you once consider me a suspect when I was in each country every time something happened?"

He watched me as I hung my head in embarrassment, knowing that the signs were all there and I missed every single one of them. He was painfully spot-on about me being so captivated by the thought of true love that I turned a blind eye to what was happening around me. I did this to myself—to my family.

"God, are you so inept. No wonder your family has no faith in you," he said to degrade me.

He continued to walk through all his treachery, step by step, delightedly pointing out how I went along with it. Like the time I danced with the Irishman and told my sisters I was leaving with a stranger for the night, when I was really meeting up with Josh. Or when I snuck him into my room on Clare Island while Mia was in the library—after he trashed the house looking for clues about the ring, he just informed me.

I believed him when he said he was at the beach processing his feelings for me right before he hopped on the ferry to the island. He claimed he was so overwhelmed with how fast our relationship was progressing, that he needed time for himself. When he heard about the break-in, he rushed to my side without the others knowing, swearing to protect me. And I bought it all.

Oh, he could tell I had an initial doubt in my mind since it was all so coincidental and our budding romance was still so new—but how persuasive he was. The lawyer in him convinced me that it would be insane of him to be so blatantly obvious, with me knowing he was in Ireland.

If he was going to be behind something like this, he wouldn't have ever shown himself to me, he said. Plus, since I thought he was back in the states when the Dublin hotel break-in happened—it was "proof" that he couldn't have possibly been behind it. So, I dropped the suspicion.

I was such an idiot to believe him.

But he hooked me good in Ireland with his leprechaun trickery. Especially after presenting me with my own Claddagh ring, declaring that even though Meg had some old family heirloom, that this would mean more because he had it created just for me, to show me how much he cared for me; how much more he cared for me than "obviously" my sisters did. He knew my Achilles heel and exploited it.

I was falling quickly for his love and his lies, that I never saw the rest coming. I felt so comfortable that I betrayed my family's secrets time after time, making it incredibly effortless for him to keep up his plan.

"Except when your bitch of a sister pulled one over on me with that decoy ring," he fumed. He reaffirmed his vow to get it back before continuing on his journey of deceit.

He thought he could make things a little easier on himself by scaring us with the notes before Italy, but we didn't take the bait, so he had to kick his strategy up a notch. He disclosed that he partnered with Dominic Moretti, who was more than happy to help a fellow con man out.

Moretti had no desire for some old jewelry box himself and thought the idea of revenge against an ancient feud line was deliciously fun, so he provided Josh with all the resources he needed to get the box back. Moretti's henchmen came in handy—as did his verification that the box was not in the attic after Josh had overheard us divulging the details in the garden cafe.

"It *was* you at the Bianchi house that day," I deduced. I knew I had seen him but told myself I was crazy; he didn't visit until a few days later when we went off on our alone time. If only I had shared my suspicion with my sisters then, instead of blowing them off, maybe this all would have turned out differently.

"I came earlier than you expected, but made you believe otherwise," he declared with glee, the sneer never leaving his face.

"Even when you questioned me, asking me if I was there, I was able to assure you that you were just seeing things—after all, you came two days later to pick me up yourself right from baggage claim at the airport," he reminded me. "Ah, that Dominic and his connections. I promised to return the favor whenever he needed it."

"So, when I called to tell you that my sisters and I were going our separate ways for a few days and I asked you to come visit, you were already in the country?" I inquired angrily, more so at myself for how gullible I had been this whole time.

"Yup," he snickered, quite pleased with himself. "It was so easy to pretend I could book a last-minute flight there. And after your little investigative questioning, I distracted you with some hot sex. Remember that beautiful 20-year-old Italian girl we picked up at the club? You gave such great head while she dined on you for dessert," he recalled wickedly.

The more he spoke, the more I was repulsed about my entire relationship with him. Every time he touched me, every lie that dripped out of his conniving mouth. If I wasn't tied up, I would beat the living shit out of this fucker. I think he sensed my fire rising, undoing his pants and bringing his hand to his cock to help it harden.

"There's the feisty spirit that gets me all hot. Do you want a little break in story time? Want some more of this?" he asked, moving towards me on the bed.

I panicked but pulled myself together to snarl at him and hit him verbally where it hurt.

"Are you so pathetic that you have to chain a woman up to have sex with her? Are you the type of gutless man who gets off on rape? That's sad."

"Rape? Fuck you, Marissa. I don't need to beg a woman for sex," he replied, clearly pissed off and backing away, his overdrawn ego evidently insulted. I hit the right button, thank God. But then he turned around to me and stuck his half-stiff dick in my face as if to put it in my mouth.

"Though I do wonder if the rush that comes along with taking a woman by force is as orgasmic as they say it is," he hinted, standing his ground. "I could always pretend we are playing dom and sub and that your begging to stop is code for fuck me harder," he said viciously.

"As if I would ever want to touch you again willingly. Fuck me if you want, but it's just my body. It means nothing to you without my resistance or my consent, because you'll get neither. It would be like doing a corpse, if you're into that sort of thing."

He considered his options for a moment before deciding to walk away, zipping his pants back up.

"So, how does your sister-in-law and her brother factor into all of this if you're estranged?" I urged him to continue, wanting to know the depths of his destructive plot.

He snickered heartily and deeply. As he unraveled more of his saga, he was becoming increasingly joyful over his great sham.

"Just collateral damage like you, sweetheart. Peggy's idiot brother had a record and I knew if I played around with his name, eventually everything would be traced back to him. I also realized that Mia's damn cop husband was good and getting too close, so I had to set someone up for the fall—and be careful about it.

"So, I kept my ticket out of Florence to New York to throw the Feds off my scent, while paying cash and hopping a plane in Pisa to Boston. I still knew that it was traceable, but by the time I had gotten through customs and hightailed it over to my nice, cushy home in Manhattan, no one would ever know it was me setting him up.

"I even gave the heads up to my stooges to reveal my 'name' on purpose if they were ever caught, knowing that it wasn't my identity the authorities would go after. In fact, that goosechase gave me the opportunity to take the fake jewelry box—thank you for spilling the beans, yet again—wrap it up as if from Jorden to Peggy and tip the cops off anonymously.

"Knowing that bitch couldn't resist a bauble, I had hoped she'd be wearing the brooch when they showed up to question her. Jesus, do I know people or what?" he snorted with triumph.

"The dumbass elitist took her sweet time thanking her brother for the gift—giving the police enough time to detain Jorden before he spoke with her. It was the perfect setup. She had no idea her brother didn't give her the box, and with his record, she thought he went way too far and was happy to give him some tough love by throwing him under the bus.

"For all his detesting that he had nothing to do with it, his past spoke for itself and he was arrested. The family foolishly confirmed her comments at the will reading, keeping her locked up as well. All that time gave me the opening to slip in the matching notepaper and have my hacker buddy craft some damning emails between them. So sweet," he uttered as he kissed his fingers Italian-style, as if every move he made was a delectable masterpiece.

"I wrote those fucking emails, yeah," he said with arrogant pride. "I planted everything. I'm a goddamn genius, Marissa; a genius that everyone underestimated.

"Oh, and I threatened to kill Peggy if her idiot brother didn't confess—but he didn't know it was me at the jail he was talking to because we never met, thanks to me being disinherited and all. You should have seen him squeal like a pig. He begged me to let Peggy go, and I agreed—if he would take the fall to clear the way for me to claim everything and get away with it.

"He knew that if he reneged or tried to claim someone else was behind it, her neck would snap like a pencil and my buddies on the inside would fuck his ass well into Tuesday.

"But the best was implanting the idea in your gullible head, little by little, that Peggy could do something like this. By the time she was arrested, you were all so eager to accept that she was the one behind it, along with her rap sheet bro—just as I expected.

"Of course, after they were detained, I realized my plan hit a snafu," he admitted with a twinge of regret. "I only had the fake ring in my possession and lost the valuable decoy that Mia set up—clever, clever, girl by the way. I have to give her props because she was hard to outsmart and made one hell of a convincing work of art.

"I had a plan to get the real ring and box like she promised in her fake note, but your damn sisters fucked that up on me again, with Meg staying in Ireland and Mia in Florence. Then when she returned, her ex-husband playing hero watching over her made it hard to get past security at her house.

"That's when I figured that I might as well wait until I get your statue from you, then while the family was in mourning and distracted, I could lift the others."

"So, with Jorden in custody, why send the threatening notes and let me believe someone was still out there?

Why not let that go and just take me here and now like you planned?"

"I did consider that. It would have made things easier to lull you into a false sense of security, but that wouldn't have been any fun. I knew how selfish you were, Marissa. I knew you would keep it a secret from your family because you wanted to come here so badly, and if you told them, they would call it off. And you couldn't have that, could you?"

He laughed as my face gave away how he was on the money.

"Told you I'm good at figuring people out," he jeered. "Oh, it was so much fucking fun to play with you. To mindfuck you. Even after I physically handed you the note, you didn't even tell *me,* your boyfriend. Classic move, Marissa. But I didn't expect you to tell that prick, Jay, by the way. Your loyalty to that jackass almost cost me everything."

"Jay…you made me believe he was behind this. But he wasn't, was he?"

"Of course not, but I had to deflect suspicion to someone, and I had it out for that meddling moron who couldn't keep his eyes off you. It gave me a hard-on to watch you tear that friendship apart. And pitting you against Bruce and causing conflict with your mom? I kept you looking everywhere but straight at me as the culprit.

"Oh, just for the record, that loser couldn't hurt a fly, he is so weak and pathetic. I'll be taking care of my buddy Bruce when I get back to the states, because he is getting a little too close for comfort for me," he noted as if making a checklist of things to do after he murdered me.

"So, what now, huh? What's the big plan now that you've got the dragon?"

"Wouldn't you like to know?"

"You're right. I don't give a fuck. You can take the statue and shove it up your ass for all I care."

Within seconds, his face was in mine again. "You should care, bitch. Because when I'm done with you, I'll be going for the others," he threatened.

"Jesus, that mouth of yours. Haven't you figured out that *you* are the reason all this is happening? If you had just kept your mouth shut and your legs open, I might have even let you go unharmed and staged some kind of break-in at our house before I dumped your ass legitimately. I would have made it work.

"But you had to push me, didn't you? You had to cross the line and bring love into this, forcing me to pretend I loved you. And now you want to do away with the kinky sex and make love.

"Moving in with you was nauseating. The only thing that kept me sane was the great sex—it's what has kept you alive all this time. You're the best little whore I've been with, and you were free," he laughed maniacally. "Well, maybe not completely free, because these trips and henchmen and strategies cost me a fortune. But now that I have the one piece, I can start making up for it."

He went over to the dragon and lifted it up, packing it into his suitcase as he gathered all his things and placed them by the door. He then brought out a red gasoline container and began dumping the fume-laced contents all over the room, concentrating by the bed.

Oh my God. He was going to light me on fire.

"You should have played nicer, Marissa," he scolded. "This all could have ended differently. But now you will burn up like the dragon you think you are. I'll just use your phone to text your location to your sisters, and then send a suicide note by email, so by the time they find you, you'll be ash in this accidental fire and they'll think both you and the damn dragon went up in flames."

"They'll never believe I killed myself, you idiot. I may be a lot of things, but I'm not suicidal. Plus, with Jay knowing about the notes, it wouldn't take long to figure out my messages were fake."

"Then I'll just have to call in another favor and make sure he has a terrible motorcycle accident before he even finds out you're dead. And then I'll have Meg mugged for her ring and tragically killed when she struggles. Unfortunate accidents. Purely coincidental.

"Oh, and my buddy in New York is ready to bound, gag and kill anyone who gets in the way of lifting the jewelry box out of Mia's hands once she gets back—maybe he'll even get to ride that ripe 16-year-old niece of yours. She's a fine piece of ass. I wouldn't mind tapping that myself," he mused.

"You're a sick bastard. I hope you rot in hell," I spat at him.

"Oh, there's that fire again that gets me hot. Yeah, that's it. Make me harder, baby. For old times' sake," he cooed, stripping down to nothing and hardening with every inch as he drew closer to me.

"You think you've won, but you haven't."

"I haven't? Tell me, Marissa—are you broken yet? Have I not obliterated every last ounce of respect you had for yourself? Destroyed your faith in men and the ability to love? Ripped your heart out of your chest?

"Think about this as you take your last breaths. Your selfish betrayal of your family has now led to your and their demise. You should be grateful that I am putting you out of your misery; you'd never be able to live with yourself. The shame, the humiliation, the grief of knowing this is all your fault."

"No, this is all the fault of an entitled psychopath. And just for the record, you didn't break me, asshole. All you did was teach me a life lesson; to listen and trust my own instincts better."

As I reviewed the flash of life before me—all the mistakes, challenges, heartaches, pain—I had never been able to see my life or myself so clearly. In my last moments, I finally understood who I was and what life was about.

"With your every attempt to bring me down, you built me up. You think your words can hurt me? You think your deceit has ruined me? You don't have that kind of power over me." It was my turn to laugh like a lunatic as he looked at me in shock.

"Sorry, buddy, but you failed. Because I still believe in love. I still believe in the goodness in the world. I still have faith in my family's forgiveness and acceptance of me for who I am—and whether they think this was suicide or murder, I know in their hearts I'll be remembered for the amazing human being I am. I am unconditionally loved by them.

"The best part? I finally respect myself, because mistakes and all, I know I am a good person. I am both the dark and the light, and I accept all parts of me. The naïve and the trusting, the vindictive and the passionate. I'm fucking fantastic just as I am. So, try as hard as you can, but you will never destroy me.

"The problem is, I was too much of a woman for you to handle. And truth be told, your dick is too small. The only reason I had to invite other men and women and fantasy tactics into our sex life was because by yourself, you didn't have what it took to pleasure me. I faked it," I revealed, knowing that if I was going down, I'd take his ego down with me.

Uh oh, that did it. I went too far, as the fury rose in him like the flames he threatened to perish me in, mounting my chained up body. I tried to resist him positioning himself to enter me, but the restraints were so tight, they almost cut off my circulation. There was nothing I could do to stop what was coming.

Deranged and lustful, with matchbox in hand, he readied himself to take whatever he wanted from my already dead body before lighting the torch.

All I could do was close my eyes and wait in agony until this nightmare was finally over.

12

"**D**on't even think about it, asshole," came the voice barreling through the cottage door, placing a 6mm gun next to Josh's head, cocked and ready to fire. "Touch her and I'll blow your fucking brains out."

"Well, well, well. Look who it is," Josh sneered as he froze in place, the cold metal pressed against his right temple.

To our absolute astonishment, there Jay stood, fierce and protective. And he wasn't kidding—he was ready to pull the trigger.

"Get off of her. Slowly," he warned. "One wrong move and I'll gladly take the electric chair in exchange for the pleasure of your death."

Josh had no choice but to concede, carefully removing himself from the bed as instructed. Jay was in soldier mode; he didn't even look at me or ask if I was all right. He was solely focused on getting this terrorist away from me.

"You think you can stop me, Boy Scout?" Josh asked in an attempt to intimidate Jay. "I have the entire cottage laced with gasoline and this match in my hand ready to strike. One wrong move and either this match—or your stray bullet—will ignite this volcano," he forewarned.

"I'll take my chances," Jay replied from behind gritted teeth. "Now move over to the door."

"And what are you going to do? Hold me here forever? You move from your position to free her, and I'll light you up and get out unharmed. You stay here like a homo up against my bare body, and she stays there, naked and chained up for you to drool over what you can't have.

"Gorgeous, isn't she? Look how perfect her breasts are. Not an ounce of fat on her toned stomach. That tight ass, man. It's everything you'd dreamed she'd be like underneath those silky nighties she wears. You should see how she writhes with pleasure when you bite her tits or ride her when she's dripping wet," he taunted.

Jay then looked over at me, trying not to notice all that Josh had pointed out as I lay there in a humiliating position.

"Shut your mouth," Jay demanded, keeping his gun on Josh's head while being careful to only look at my face and make eye contact as he spoke to me.

"Are you okay? Did he hurt you?"

"No. You got here just in time. How did you find me?"

Before Jay could answer, Josh took the distracted opportunity to move away and light the match, threatening to drop it near me.

"Looks like we're at a draw, partner," Josh teased condescendingly.

"No, we're not," Jay countered, and in an instant, the battle was over.

Jay fired a single, perfect shot to Josh's groin, dropping him and his match to the ground—thankfully in a spot where the idiot had very little gasoline. Some kind of angel had to have stepped in to make sure of that. Jay was able to swiftly stop the spark of fire that started in the carpet as his victim lay in a small pool of blood, grasping his damaged penis in groaning agony.

Knowing he didn't have much time before Josh could possibly get up, Jay moved to the bed to first cover my exposed body with a sheet, and then released me from the chains. Keeping the gun pointed at Josh with one hand, he brought me against his chest with the other.

"I'm so glad you are okay," he murmured, placing kisses all over my face and leaning his forehead into mine with a deep sigh. "I would never have forgiven myself if anything had happened to you." He hugged me tighter, then released me when he felt some of the sheet slip away; my bare breasts pressing up against his chest.

"You should put some clothes on. The cops will be here soon," he said, blushing and turning away to give me privacy.

Everything that happened afterwards was a blur. As promised, the authorities were on the scene within minutes, as well as an ambulance and armed escorts to take the injured Josh to the hospital. Unfortunately, the scumbag would live; not so sure his cock would, though. The thought of him never being able to have sex again brought an evil smile to my face. *Way to go, Jay.*

The next few hours were spent being interrogated by the police, as I reiterated Josh's list of crimes and motives verbatim to them, as well as to Jay and my sisters, who met up with me at the station with hugs of relief. The police also questioned Jay in a separate room before clearing him of all charges, ultimately declaring the gunshot was in self-defense. He wouldn't have to spend a single day in international jail, thanks to Bruce's calls and connections.

EJ came storming in shortly after, and gratefully, my sisters took on the job of bringing him up to speed so I did not have to relive the nightmare again. I was in a daze, drinking down glasses of water shoved in my face, accepting embraces from everyone around me and repressing the trauma I had just been through. I didn't even notice that we were back at the villa, and I was in my room.

I can't believe I survived that. It was a miracle.

A light knock at my door brought me back to the present. Meg and Mia quietly entered and sat down on the bed beside me.

"How are you doing, honey?" Meg asked.

"I'm okay, I guess. It's a lot to process," I said stoically.

"You've been through quite an ordeal. Is there anything we can do for you?" Mia asked, grabbing my hand while Meg rubbed my back.

"Do you know where my phone is?"

"It's right here on the night stand. Jay grabbed all your stuff when you left the cottage. The police currently have the statue from Josh's bag in evidence right now, but they assured us they would return it in the morning."

"Okay," I answered, looking at my phone to see the countless missed calls and texts from my loved ones trying to track me down.

"How did you know I was in danger?"

"It all happened so quickly," Mia began. "After Jay wasn't able to get in touch with you, he called to alert me about Josh, hoping that I was with you and could watch over you until he got here. I tried to reach you to warn you, but you must have turned your ringer off.

"Not even five minutes later, EJ called to tell me about the note you left behind for him, and how the guards said you went off with some guy matching Josh's description with the promise you would be safe, and it took me all of one second to figure out that he got to you before we did.

"We were so terrified that we lost you," cried Mia.

"I'm so sorry," I broke down, allowing the sobs to flow out of me. My chest hurt as I heaved, the excruciating pain of betrayal and disbelief over being rescued consuming me. My sisters sheltered me in their bear hug sandwich, the tears also pouring down their faces as we wept together.

"I should have been honest about Josh all along. If I had, one of you would have been smart enough to catch on to his plan long before this," I confessed.

"If you had only known he had snuck on our trips to Ireland and Italy to spend time with me, and that I was spilling my guts to him more than I let on, we likely wouldn't even be in this mess. I should've told you about the recent threats. I shouldn't have been selfish, putting us all in danger over some stupid statue," I admitted in defeat.

"Don't do that to yourself," Meg hushed. "Don't blame yourself. You did what you thought was right at the time. We're just relieved that you weren't hurt. That's all that matters."

"Besides," Mia added, "we might have done the same thing in your shoes. But I will say I am glad you confided in Jay about everything. He's the one who figured it all out, and the reason you're breathing right now."

"Where is he?" I asked, wanting to see my dear, brave friend.

"He's patiently sitting with EJ by the pool, waiting to see you. He wanted us to make sure you were up for a visit before he bothered you."

"Bothered me? He saved my life. How could he even think that?"

"That's what we said," Meg chuckled. "Should I let him know that you'd like to see him?"

"Yes, please," I smiled up at them. Before they could

leave, I stopped them and gave them each a hug. "Thank you for being the best sisters in the entire world. I love you so much and promise to never let another day go by without telling you again."

"We love you, too," they replied in unison.

I stood up to look in the mirror. I aged about twenty years from lack of sleep and stress. I must have looked like a horror film with my gaping zombie eyes and drooping cheeks. My dirty, unwashed hair and the thought of Josh's DNA still on and in me almost made me vomit in my mouth.

I had to get into the shower and wash away the filth; scrub the horrific memories off my body and out of my mind. By the time I was done, my skin was almost raw from panicked exfoliation. I was grateful he never got to rape me, but he was still a part of me—a part I needed to flush and forget.

Stepping outside into the bedroom in a towel, I had forgotten that Jay was on his way in. He swallowed hard in embarrassment, excusing himself towards the door and promising to come back at a better time so I could get myself dressed.

"No, wait," I said. "Stay. I'll get changed in the bathroom and be right out."

Like a nervous teenager, Jay sat in the corner in the oversized lounge chair, his hands wringing together as his leg bounced up and down in his classically anxious way.

"Hi," I started, alerting him that I was fully dressed and present.

"Hi," he simply responded, not knowing what else to say. I motioned for him to come sit on the bed next to me, so we could talk. He reluctantly settled beside me, finding it difficult to look me in the eyes.

"Thank you," I managed, reaching my arms out to him, bringing him close to me as he let out his own cries of relief now that the nightmare was over.

"I'm sorry I didn't get here sooner. I'm sorry I failed to protect you like I promised."

"Jay, look at me," I said lifting his chin up so that we could be face-to-face. "You did exactly as you promised," I assured him. "I am here, alive and unharmed, because of you. By the way, how did you find me?"

"Location tracker," he confessed. "Remember a few months ago when we went to the Coldplay concert and we shared our locations on our phones in case we got separated?"

I nodded in recollection—that was a kickass concert, too.

"Well, you never turned your location sharing off from me. Once I landed and learned you were missing, I checked my phone and miraculously, wherever you were had the reception I needed to find you."

"So, how did you figure out Josh was behind it all?"

"It's a long story."

"No time like the present," I responded, sitting back onto the bed and pulling him to me into a comfortable position, my head on his familiar and safe shoulders. "Let's hear it."

It all began when I asked him to keep an eye on Bruce. Well, actually earlier than that, because Jay had always had his suspicions that Josh was up to no good, but didn't have anything concrete enough to prove it. He only had the information (lies) Josh told me to go on, and since it was agreed that he had plausible alibis the whole time, there was no need to question the "facts" and accuse him.

Knowing that I was way too into the guy, Jay didn't bring up the subject anymore and privately kept notes on what I told him in hopes of figuring out what my boyfriend was really up to.

Wanting to find out the truth behind Bruce's ominous 'watch your back' warning, Jay reached out to him to set up that meeting at the coffee shop.

"I'm sorry for not telling you about that, Riss, but I knew you kept feeding information to Josh. It's not that I didn't trust you. I just couldn't risk you tipping him or anyone else off about what I was up to," he reasonably explained.

"Given the circumstances, I get it now. I'm glad you followed your gut—at least one of us did. I'm just sorry you had to endure my wrath," I offered apologetically.

"It was worth it to see you safe," he said, and meant it. But there was much more to the story he had yet to reveal.

When Jay and Bruce talked, they ended up exchanging information—Jay about my threatening note and Bruce's ill-timed wording, and Bruce about his investigative file on Josh and the Marinos. Turns out, my mother's man had his own antenna up in protection of his love and her daughters.

Since they did, in fact, move in the same professional circles, while Josh was trying to discredit Bruce in my eyes, Bruce was diligently gathering intel on Joshua Pekins. So far, he had only learned that Josh was on probation for attempting to bribe a judge, getting off with a warning. That wasn't enough for them to lynch him just yet.

Bruce then approached Kevin one night while helping with a security camera installation, triggered by a gut feeling that something was awry about Jorden and Peggy being arrested. It just so happened that Kevin was suspicious all along as well—too clean of a capture to not question if it was a setup.

But for our safety and peace of mind, both men agreed to play along with the scenario that the duo was guilty, while hatching a plan to have Bruce represent Peggy. Kevin thought that if he could earn Peggy's trust, he could investigate the skeletons in the Marino family without tipping off the real perpetrator.

But Peggy was released before Bruce could learn anything new, and we were already en route to Spain, so there was nothing he could do to stop us—except try to warn me to be careful, which I mistook for a threat.

Bruce was glad to receive the call from Jay, as he had hit a dead end. After their coffee shop meeting and Jay's brilliant idea to go back to the Marino drawing board, Bruce requested a meeting with Peggy, who was more than willing to open up to her new lawyer once she found out he could help free her innocent brother. Apparently, she had a change of heart about the scoundrel and didn't believe he would be more than a "harmless" drug dealer.

It didn't take long for Peggy to reveal that Patrick had an estranged younger brother who changed his last name to Perkins. At the same time, Kevin learned that a blonde-haired lawyer type visited Jorden in jail—igniting the lightbulb that prompted the connection between my boyfriend and the disowned heir.

That's when Jorden finally revealed the threat against his sister and proclaimed his innocence once again. But since Josh had never revealed his identity to Jorden, the police still had more work to do to tie him to the crime and make an arrest. The cameras never caught his face, so they had no hard evidence that it was Josh who really visited Jorden.

Shortly after, one of Kevin's associates tracked down the closed juvenile records of Joshua Marino, which uncovered his allegedly accidental, drug-related stabbing that killed another young boy, for which he spent time in a correctional detention center.

Even though this was an underage crime with sealed records, Josh didn't mind the forced family name change and brand new start as a Perkins, enabling him to become a dirty lawyer with access to all kinds of underground resources to support his criminal pursuits—including a fake identity passport procured with Jorden's altered name, using Josh's photo, and then a second one with Jorden's real photo to plant as dummy evidence.

"Josh really did think of everything," I mused solemnly.

Once Bruce filled Jay in on this newly revealed information, my best friend booked a red eye to come find me. They knew time was of the essence, seeing as the tail Kevin had put on Josh lost him earlier in the day, and Bruce confirmed he had no court hearings on the docket. Then, panic set in when no one was able to get ahold of me.

"That's when all the pieces were starting to come together that Josh was truly behind it all, and that you were in grave danger. By the time I landed, he had already kidnapped you and we feared it was too late."

I shook my head in disbelief.

"All the signs were there," I admitted. "Not just the obvious ones, like him being in the countries when the break-ins happened. I mean, the subtle signs. Who else would know that Meg's ring was hidden in a Fabergé egg in the little church where the priest was called? That we had a feuding line of Bianchis who could have possession of the jewelry box and be the perfect accomplices? That there were real items versus decoy items, for heaven's sake?"

"Technically…me. You did share all of that with me, too."

"Oh, you're right. I did have loose lips," I confessed, embarrassed again that I fell into the trap and endangered everyone I loved. "Huh, all this time, he had me thinking you or Bruce were in cahoots with the Marinos, when it was him all along. He actually had me doubting *you,*" I looked at him apologetically.

"It's okay, Riss. The guy is a master manipulator. He had your heart and your trust. I don't blame you for wanting to believe your boyfriend. Even though I've known you your whole life," he joked to lighten the mood. I had to laugh along with him.

"So, what did he say that made you doubt me, anyway?"

"Well, first it was him spotting you with Bruce—and then when you failed my little tests to get the information out of you, it made his whole story more believable about me not being able to trust you. I thought it might have something to do with the scheme you were hiding from me when we got into our fight."

"Oh that? I, uh, was ashamed that I got involved in some pyramid sales funnel thing that almost wiped out my savings and was freaking out that I wouldn't be able to pay the rent and let you down. Plus, I got some of my buddies involved who were on the verge of losing money as well, so I had to set things right."

"That's it? *That's* what you were hiding from me? Are

you kidding?" I asked disbelievingly.

"There's a lot more to that story, but we don't need to get into that right now," he said, shifting nervously with body language that begged "not now," and yet, nothing that screamed anything more than poor, impulsive decision making on his part. Definitely not sinister or malice; just stupidity.

"Okay, fine. But you're not getting out of it, mister," I warned with a light finger wave. "Oh yeah—he also told me he investigated you and found out you were college best friends with his nephew, Thomas Marino."

"Thomas Marino? Dude, I've never even heard of the guy."

"Well, I believe that now," I said groggily, feeling the weight of my eyelids bog me down.

"Okay, Riss. You've had enough. I should go and let you rest now."

"No, please don't go," I pleaded. "I don't want to be alone."

"Okay," he said hesitantly, as I snuggled into his warm, comforting, trusting arms and fell fast asleep.

Jay must have been as tired as I was, because we woke up side-by-side, still in each other's arms, on top of the bed covers as the morning light snuck in through a crack in the blinds. I looked up at him, feeling loved and protected, finally seeing what everyone has been trying to tell me for years.

No one has ever loved me the way Jay has.

But I couldn't think about that now, coming off a long ordeal with a few more days ahead of me until this was finally over.

Today, everyone was somber, the gravity of these last few months finally taking a toll on all the game players. Ever the spirit-lifter, a loud, Hawaiian shirt-wearing EJ swung into the kitchen where we all sat drinking coffee and announced that he had the perfect day planned for us—a quiet day at the beach.

At first, we started to resist, but he insisted that the moping would only get worse if we confined ourselves to this stiff little villa. Knowing that none of us could successfully talk him down off the pep squad ledge, we gave in and let him take us to a quiet little seashore on the outskirts of the city—with fully dressed beach-goers, thank goodness.

The fresh air did us all some good. With our family slated to fly in tomorrow, it really was a smart idea to soak up what was left of the peace.

I welcomed the burn of the sun on my back, enjoying the heat and stillness. Meg, Mia and EJ preferred to dive right into the water, but I wasn't quite in the mood to move from my secluded spot. Jay opted to stay behind to watch over me like a guard dog, despite my protests that he should go enjoy himself.

"Go. I'm fine. I promise."

"So am I. The view is spectacular. With everything that went down yesterday, it's just hitting me now that I'm in Spain. I'm actually on the Mediterranean coast. How wild is that?"

"Pretty wild," I indulged him, twisting my neck back and forth as I felt a cramp creep in.

"You okay?"

"Yeah, it's just my neck is so stiff."

"I'm not surprised with how long that lunatic kept you chained up in that awkward position. Here, let me help," he offered, sitting up so that he could rub out the tension that plagued my neck.

I'm not going to lie, it felt incredible. His hands skillfully and deeply massaged the knots of my neck and I encouraged him with my body language to continue down to my equally locked up shoulders and back.

He poured some of the sunscreen onto his hands as a lubricative buffer, gently and methodically pressing along my tightest areas to relieve the pent-up stress. If he didn't make it as a musician, he could definitely make a killing as a massage therapist.

Although he was being quite professional about it, I could feel the sensuality behind each stroke; an affection behind each healing motion.

"That feels incredible," I said, not realizing it came out as a sexually-induced moan. I felt his hands instantly freeze up, their fluidity becoming rigid as he quickly finished up.

"There. That better?"

"Much. Why did you stop?" I turned to ask him.

"Oh, I was getting a cramp in my hand. Sorry," he said, lying unsuccessfully. How respectfully cute of him. I'd let it go for now.

"I'm going to just run up to the bar. Want me to grab you a drink?" I nodded emphatically, knowing I could use something more to keep the nerves at bay.

A few minutes later, he was back with a few bottles of beer and a plate of nachos.

"So, your mom and everyone is coming in tomorrow, huh?" he said, sadly trying to make uncomfortable small talk. He was even more adorable when he was geeky.

"Well, Mom, Granny and Bruce get in tonight after dinner—oh, and EJ's husband, Rodney, too. Colleen and

Kieran fly in together in the morning and will probably meet up with Francesco at the airport arriving around the same time."

"So, what's the plan? I know the big party is at night, but what's going on during the day?"

"I don't know exactly. I'm pretty sure Meg and Kieran will want some alone time, and I have a feeling that Mia might end up in Francesco's hotel room for a little catchup rendezvous," I giggled. "With all that has gone on, just to be safe, the kids are going to stay behind with Kevin in New York. So, she'll *carpe diem* the hell out of that opportunity."

"What about you?"

"Well, EJ said something about taking Rodney, Mom, Bruce, Granny and Colleen on an expedited tour of Barcelona while the party planners decorate the house and set up the feast. I was thinking I could join them and spend a little time with my mom. You wanna come?"

"Sure," he said, hesitation masking his feigned excitement.

"Okay, what's wrong?"

"Nothing. Sounds great."

"Jay, I know you better than that. What is it?"

"Well, I was just thinking...maybe you might want to take a ride with me at some point. I reserved a bike for the morning and was going to ride the countryside. I thought, I don't know, possibly we could go together? But I get you want to see your mom, so maybe some other time."

"Are you joking? I love that idea!" I exclaimed. "EJ took me on a ride up to the raceway circuit the other day and it was unbelievable. I'd love to explore some more of the country with you."

"But what about your family?"

"You can't dangle a motorcycle carrot in front of me and expect me to turn that down! Besides, I'm not sure how much family togetherness I can take once everyone arrives," I chuckled—but meant it. "We can plan to spend the morning on our own tour and then meet up with everyone for siesta in the afternoon. Best of both worlds. How does that sound?"

"Great," he beamed like a little kid, sitting back into the sand with the first genuine smile I've seen on his face since he arrived. After that, we both were ready to jump up and join the others in the water and spend the rest of the afternoon lounging amidst relaxed chatter.

Dinner was a magnificent fanfare overlooking the water, as EJ, of course, had to show off his now polished Catalonian culinary expertise for our newest guest. Tapas galore lined our table, along with pitchers of sangria.

"A toast," he began as we raised our glasses in anticipation of what our cousin had to say. "To three very brave, extraordinary women. You are all gutsy, inspirational and an absolute pleasure to be around. It is an honor to call you family. Cheers."

"Cheers!"

"And to two incredible men, without whom I would not be here today. I love you both so much," I added.

"To family and friends," Mia summated.

"To family and friends," we echoed.

13

I had never been so happy to see my mother in my entire life. The moment she walked through the door, I ran straight into her arms.

"Oh, my baby girl," she cried, holding me as tight as I held her. "I'm so happy to see you. How are you doing, sweetheart?"

"Much better now that you're here. It was so awful, Mom."

"I can't even imagine," she said as she took my face in her hands and stared as if she needed to memorize every inch of it. "I'm so sorry I wasn't there for you."

"Don't be silly. You couldn't have known," I replied.

"But I should have," came the mousy, fragile, tired voice of my beloved grandmother. "I shouldn't have fallen for his cheap charm. Guess old dogs can't learn new tricks after all."

"Oh, Granny." I left my mother's arms to tightly squeeze and kiss her. "I love you. But it wasn't your fault either. It wasn't anyone's. He swindled all of us."

"Not all," interjected Bruce in a playful tone, who came out from behind Granny, his hands full of luggage. He stood there awkwardly smiling, unsure of how to greet me given the aloofness of our past interactions. I ended the doubt as soon as I walked over and threw my arms around him.

"Thank you," I whispered in his ear.

"It was nothing," he gushed, showing his shy side. "I'm just glad it all worked out in the end. How are you holding up, kiddo?"

"I'm better. It's still surreal to me. But knowing that son of a bitch is chained to a hospital bed and headed to jail helps."

"And if I have anything to do with it, he'll be there a very long time," he added. "In fact, he's already been extradited back to the U.S. and Jorden has been released. Which reminds me—thanks to your statement and permission, we got the search warrant for Josh's house. Guess he didn't realize that living with you would give us the access we needed to take him down.

"We were able to locate his hidden desk drawer in that studio he set up for you. In it was a black leather-bound book filled with his intricate plan that corroborated your story and every person he had contact with, including their role. Kevin and his team were able to track every single one of them down, get a statement and diffuse them. No one will be coming after any of you anymore.

"Including Dominic Moretti, who is also now in custody on several counts, thanks to Josh's written elaborations of his corruptive history and a paper trail to follow. Everyone's crimes were wrapped in a neat, thorough little package. Right down to the tax evasions and drug smuggling," he beamed.

"How could we ever repay you for helping us, Bruce?" Mia asked.

"Mia, you don't ever have to repay me. That's what family is for. Besides, Kevin and Jay played a big part as well. I think we make a very good Three Musketeers," he said with pride.

"We certainly do," agreed Jay as he walked into the room, along with Rodney, who was the last to enter. "EJ's been busy in the kitchen and asked me to come welcome you all. Who's up for some tea?"

We gathered in the living room, a renewed energy with the entrance of our special visitors. We took turns catching up: I filled them in on the details of what happened with Josh; Mom gave Mia an update on the kids; Granny told us all about her casino winnings from her last trip; EJ and Rodney shared an adorable reunion talking about Muffy, their dog; and Meg and Mia finally had the chance to regale their stories about their quite entertaining journey through France.

As we wound down for the evening, we realized we needed to figure out the best sleeping arrangements for our newest guests, though of course, our "host with the most" cousin already had it mapped out.

Meg would move in with Mia for now, giving Mom and Bruce the privacy of her room. EJ insisted that Granny have his room; the futon he had set up in the art studio was more than adequately comfortable for him and his love, he declared. Jay was going to create his own man cave on the couch, but I insisted that he stayed with me.

"No, Riss, it's fine. You need your own space. I'm totally okay here."

"What's the big deal? We slept together last night."

The whole room turned and looked at me, as I realized what I said didn't come out right. It didn't stop Jay from turning fifty shades of crimson though.

"Oh, no—not like that," I back-peddled. "I just meant—we just happened to fall asleep together. I—I don't want to be alone," I looked at him and knew he couldn't say no to my pleading eyes—the same ones that reluctantly earned me a ride on his bike that final morning as roommates together.

"Fine. But I'm sleeping on the floor," he insisted.

He didn't. I manipulated him into joining me in bed. I needed to feel the safety of his presence beside me. Even though I knew Josh was locked up, I hadn't quite released the fear that he'd come back for me. Telling him that had him snuggled up and ready to protect me in an instant.

Men really are so easy to figure out at times—now that I had a clue that this particular man was legit.

Waking up in his arms for the second morning in a row felt so natural that I didn't even notice I kissed him good morning until he jolted up after a sensuous response.

"Wait—what are you doing?"

"Oh my God. I am so—sorry. Force of habit I guess," I suggested, embarrassed beyond all belief.

"Oh. I, um, I'm going to grab a shower before everyone gets here," he croaked out, rising from the bed and avoiding any further talk about what had just happened—or how his morning wood was standing at attention.

Damn, he really was a fine-looking man, even with his facial scruff and disheveled head of thick hair. *Stop it, Marissa,* I scolded myself. *You just ended a relationship with a serial narcissist not even two days ago. Must you always think about sex?*

The morning was bustling, as one by one our cousins arrived. First came Francesco, whose flight landed earlier than expected. After greeting the family, he unapologetically whisked Mia away for a day at the Gardens of Mossèn Cinto Verdaguer, promising to have her back in plenty of time for the party. I loved the way my sister glowed with anticipation of a heavenly day in nature with an old, sexy beau.

Next came the raucous arrival of lovable Colleen, chattering up a storm in her adorable Irish tongue. Entering behind her was dear Kieran, courteously greeting us all hello before running to his love and lifting her off her feet in a sweeping circle. Seeing them together after all the heartaches she's endured gave me hope that one day, I could find that kind of true love.

It was now Kieran's turn to steal Meg away for a romantic Spanish getaway, with another oath that they would be back in time for the festivities.

That left Colleen and EJ to happily reacquaint themselves after their introductions last year when Leigh set his whole plan in motion. Hugs abound as Colleen greeted her other American kin, inviting them to come to the O'Sullivan house anytime they pleased.

"Thank you so much," Mom replied. "We would love that."

"Ah, sure look it. It'd be grand to have you there," our cousin beamed. "So, what's the story?"

Since I was the only one left who was most fluent in "Colleen," I took the lead.

"EJ wanted to take you all on a master tour of Barcelona, to some of his favorite spots. If it's all right with you, Jay and I are going to take a morning motorcycle ride and will meet you around lunchtime."

"Of course, sweetheart," permitted my mother graciously. "Enjoy your ride."

"Fabulous," exclaimed our tour guide cousin. "I'm figuring we'll be by Las Ramblas by one-ish. You know, I thought I'd take them to our fave little tapas place."

"Sounds perfect, cuz. We'll see you then," I said, giving everyone a big kiss goodbye and grabbing Jay by the hand to start our adventure. He looked smoking in his blue jeans and black leather jacket—funny how we ended up twinning with the same exact outfit, right down to the white button down shirt and black boots.

"Hop on," he said, handing me a black helmet with pink stripes after I pulled my hair back into a messy but effective braid.

"Duh, aren't I supposed to get on after you?"

"Not today," he grinned. "Today, you'll be doing the driving."

"Are you serious?" I squealed, unable to contain my excitement.

Always the companion, never the rider, it killed me that I could never take the lead. No way would Jay ever let me on his baby, just like every other man who denied me the opportunity.

I couldn't believe he was actually going to let me drive. Me. Marissa Rossi. I was going to steer us along the Spanish coastline.

After a few quick lessons and practice runs around the villa driveway, he gave me the green light to take off to anywhere my heart desired.

I don't think I will ever be satisfied riding as a passenger again. The power of holding on to the Harley's love handles electrified all the cells in my body. The thrill of rolling the throttle fueled both me and the bike as we cruised away, hearing nothing but the symphony of the grueling engine. Clutching the bike with my legs as they molded perfectly to my thighs gave me a whole new appreciation for being on top.

Some people find their center in a twisted yoga position; I meditate on the open road. All the tension and fears from the terror with Josh blew away in the gusts of wind that carried us on paved clouds.

My genetic code was programmed for this kind of life.

After an hour of riding without a single word spoken, I pulled over to this small, secluded park overlooking the water. We dismounted, remaining silent, as I took his hand in mine and led him to sit on the dry, browning grass beside me.

"That was the best PTSD therapy I could have ever received," I sighed, knowing that when I returned, I did need to make a real appointment to talk through and heal my trauma with a professional. I couldn't resolve this one on my own; I owed it to myself and to my loved ones to get the care I needed to move forward with my life. But this moment right here was certainly a good start.

We continued to watch the glistening waves in the distance, the birds flying in and around a clear sky, not needing to say anything further.

My chest was lighter, and I could feel my breath restore to its natural state. I absentmindedly leaned back and into Jay's chest, closing my eyes and letting our lungs work in rhythmic unison. A few moments later, he shifted his body and my head ended up in his lap, his fingers mindlessly stroking my hair. I could feel him progressively tense with every relaxed touch.

"Riss, I need to talk to you about something." His legs started to tremble as I lifted my head and body to sit up and give him my full attention.

"It sounds serious."

"It is." He was struggling to formulate the words, taking three deep breaths to calm his erratic nerves.

"I'll never forget what I walked in on the other day. Seeing you like that. Degraded, abused. It took a lot of restraint not to instantly pull the trigger," he admitted, holding his finger up to my lips before I could respond. "Please, just let me get this out.

"It made me think about how I pinned you up against the wall the day I moved out. How I could have hurt you just because I was angry. I haven't forgiven myself for that," he said, hanging his head in shame. "But I thought you deserved to know what triggered me that night."

He was finally ready to talk, and I was ready to listen.

"We've known each other since we were kids, Riss. From the moment we met, we were like these badass kindred spirits."

"Peanut butter and jelly." I couldn't help interrupting, fondly reminiscing what we called ourselves in our youth. "You, of course, being the smooth one, and me the sweet and flavorful one."

"Flavorful I'll give you; sweet—let's circle back on that one," he teased as I good-humoredly pushed him away before resuming my attentive state.

"Anyway, back then, we were just these dorky, troublemaking PB&J kids. I was drawn to your feisty, free spirit, but I've always known you to be more than that. I've watched you compare yourself to your sisters your entire life, and it bothers me that you don't see what I see.

"You have intelligence and ambition in spades. You're the girl who when she got an 'F' on her history essay in the eighth grade for not responding to the question correctly, confronted the teacher and persuaded her that an alternative perspective was absolutely acceptable. You got your 'A' because that's what you do—you never back down.

"You're the girl who saw an awkward little classmate cornered by the swing sets near a bunch of bullies and fearlessly knocked each one of them on their asses with your fist, but then took that sweet girl by the hand and started skipping with her. You and Em are still friends today because of that moment.

"You helped a lost little bird find its nest; were the first in line to help care for your dying Pops Mahoney after his stroke; and you took your wool coat off in the middle of a frigid New York City afternoon to give it to a cold homeless person. You have one of the biggest hearts I know.

"You have this passion that is unsurpassed. Sometimes it's sassiness; sometimes it's sexual confidence; and sometimes it's artistic brilliance. You have been this way ever since I've known you as a spunky little brat with an overbite, and I've admired and respected you for it every single day of my life."

"You saw me before I was beautiful," I finally grasped.

"Correction: I *always* saw you as beautiful."

"Why are you telling me all this now?"

"Because I wanted you to know why you were impossible to live with."

"Wait, what? You pretty much told me how fabulous you think I am, but not as a roommate?" He laughed as I looked at him puzzled. That had to be the worst backhanded compliment anyone has ever given me.

"Oh, you silly, sensitive girl," he teased, finding great amusement in my perplexion. "You are fine as a roommate—except when you walk around in your see-through lingerie and make me listen to hours of you having sex with your boyfriend."

"Oh. Well, if I promise to be more considerate, do you think we could be roommates again?"

"You really are daft sometimes, girl. Why do you

think I got so angry that night?"

"I honestly don't know."

"Marissa Rossi, I have loved you since I was eight years old," his confession began. "We've spent our formative years screwing up our love lives with all these awful relationships. Somewhere along the way, a few years ago, I realized that the woman I've been searching for all my life was *you.*

"The girl I told you about, the unavailable one who treated me like just a friend? The one you would tell me wasn't worth it and that I should get over her? It was you all along, Riss. My jealousy had reached its breaking point and I couldn't torture myself anymore by seeing you day in and day out as just my best friend.

"Don't get me wrong—I can accept you as my best friend, if that is all you will ever see me as—but I just can't live in the same space with you anymore without giving in to temptation and ruining almost thirty years of friendship.

"Being here with you, waking up with you, has been both wonderful and painful. Even right now, as I'm spilling my guts out to you, all I want to do is kiss you and never let you go.

"But I know you have been through a terrible ordeal and you have a lot of healing to do. I'm not pressuring you to react or love me back or any of it. I'm not trying to dump this all on you with an ulterior motive.

"I just needed to come clean because I don't want there to be any more lies or secrets between us. You mean the world to me, Riss. You need to know that I am right here for you, however you want me to be, to get you through this and any other challenge that comes your way."

I didn't know what to say. I felt like I should respond,

but words escaped me. Like, part of me deep down knew how he really felt all along, especially when my sisters pointed it out. I denied it, but I knew why he had to move out of our apartment, and it broke my heart.

It broke my heart because I think I was feeling the same way all along, but pushed it down because I was committed to Josh.

I started to speak, but he just shook his head.

"You don't have to say anything," he reassured me, relief washing over both of us that this was finally out in the open and no longer tearing at us. "I'd rather you not force a nicety out to spare my feelings or say something you might not mean. When the words want to come, I'll listen."

And with that, he kissed the top of my forehead and led me back to the bike.

Lunch at Las Ramblas was quite the spectacle, with EJ and Rodney hooting and hollering over drinks, Colleen getting up to dance and my family laughing heartily in response to their antics. What a crazy family I had accumulated over this last year—and I wouldn't trade a single one of them.

Since we arrived separately by motorcycle instead of the clown car the rest of the gang traveled in, Jay and I were able to weave in and out of traffic and arrive back at the villa much sooner than everyone else. Even though it pained me to give up control, I thought Jay could use some reflective driving time of his own on the way back. I'm sure it couldn't have been easy on him to share his feelings with me and not get a response.

The party planners were hurried little carpenter ants,

bringing in tables, floral centerpieces and Lord knows whatever other over-the-top ideas EJ had in store for us. Not wanting to get in the way, I thought it would be a good time to show Jay my latest paintings.

"They are fantastic! They're so—you!"

"Really?"

"Of course. They've got your fiery passion and are unapologetically bold and honest. I love these so much more than your landscapes—no offense," he quickly added.

"Wow, thank you. EJ said the same thing. He wants to put them on display in his gallery when we get back."

"For real? That's amazing! I'm so proud of you!" he screamed as he picked me up and spun me around. "My girl's an artist!"

"Your girl, huh?"

"Well, you know what I mean. My bestie girl," he covered nervously.

"That's not what you meant." There was no use in playing games. I couldn't help but see him in a different light since his confession—no, since his rescue. It made what happen next feel so right.

I leaned up to kiss him, wrapping my hands around his neck to bring him closer to me. Surprised and slow to respond, I urged him with my lips to open up to me, finally granting him the permission to cross that line from friend to lover.

I never knew a kiss could be so gentle, so sweet, so endearing. Even when our tongues met, he was tender and soft, even reserved—wanting to cherish this moment as if it would be the only time our lips would ever meet. His hands cupped my face as we explored, tasted and delighted in the coming together of the old friendship and the new possibilities.

"Riss…" He searched my face, still so unsure if what we were doing was the right thing.

"No. My turn to talk," I commanded lightly. "Before the incident with Josh, I had an epiphany—well, a number of them, actually. These paintings reflect what has been hidden in me for so long. EJ helped me see that, and so did my dragon statue and so many other people in my life who love me, including you.

"For as long as I can remember, I've been in a one-way competition with my sisters, always wishing I could 'one-up' them. But we are all the sun and the shadow; each one of us has our own strengths and weaknesses—and together we are stronger.

"I will no longer deny that I have both darkness and light within me; I am not afraid to be who I am, and I will not change for anyone. But what I will do is free my gifts from their chains and honor the goodness in me. I have so much potential to unleash upon the world, and it's ready for me."

I moved on to the next painting, demonstrating to Jay that I had a story to tell for each one and needed a captive audience. He respectfully stood in silence, following my lead.

"In trying to use sex as a weapon to control men, it backfired on me, giving men the power to use sex against me. Men just wanted one thing from me, and the only way I could get approval or acceptance or work my way up the artistic ladder was through my body instead of what I really had to offer.

"I no longer want that kind of game in my life. My body is a temple and a gift, and I won't be giving of it lightly," I hinted. He smiled in obvious respect for my decision as he moved back around me, his arms enveloping my waist and his chin lightly resting on my shoulder.

"Love," I sighed, running my fingers around the dragon-burnt heart. "I used to think it was impossible for me. That I was never good enough to deserve the love of a good, honorable man who would want more than my physical beauty.

"You would think that what Josh did to me would have scarred me for life; and in many ways, it has. I won't easily forget that betrayal or walk confidently without looking over my shoulder. At least, not for a while. But he did not destroy me. I will not give him that satisfaction of burning my heart to a crisp.

"Quite the contrary; his attempt to break me made me even more defiant. I don't want to shut down, Jay. I want to keep my heart open and loving and completely vulnerable. You make me feel safe, protected and cherished." I turned around to face him, meeting him eye-to-eye with a depth I never allowed myself to express.

"I have loved you for as long as you have loved me. But, I'm not ready to walk down that path just yet. I want—*need*—to take things slow. I don't know when I will be able to share my body so intimately after what I just experienced. I can't make you any promises, Jay, other than to take it one moment at a time."

The way he looked at me crushed my soul…in the best of ways. Real, raw, true. My musical poet.

"I have waited decades to be with you, Riss. I can wait decades more, because you are so much more than a body. You are my soulmate. I want you to be my forever," he replied, bending slowly down for a short but deeply affectionate kiss to assure me that he accepted my terms and wasn't going anywhere.

I was tempted to dive deeper into this moment when the noise level of the house hit the roof with the entry of my boisterous family members—Colleen taking the lead.

"Shall we get ready for the party?" Jay asked as he regretfully removed himself from our romantic hold to be honorable.

"Let's do it."

14

An arc of gold and silver balloons lined the entranceway to the rooftop pool. Tables were laced with glittery cloths and chairs with sparkling bows. Centerpieces of bright red carnations and Catalonia's national golden weaver's broom flowers burst out of clear glass vases.

Waiters in contemporary tuxedos with red bowties stood in stance with trays lined with doilies—some with glasses of cava, others with assorted tapas. Flamenco-style music escorted us back to our evening in Madrid as hired dancers glided across the far side of the pool.

"You've outdone yourself, EJ. This is extraordinary," Meg said.

"Only the best for my favorite cousins," he declared. "So, who's ready for the grand finale?"

He brought us over to a beautiful altar-like display, with large framed photographs of who I rightfully assumed were our grandfather, Leigh, and great-grandmother, Lena. He gestured to Colleen and Francesco to join him in front, presenting them each with our heirlooms that he had gathered back for this evening.

"I would like to start off by saying when Leigh first approached me to fulfill his wishes, I thought he was battier than Robin," EJ began. "But as time went on, and I saw his plan unfold, I have never been more in awe of a man's vision before in my life. He truly was a genius whose heart was used for good in the end.

"As we stand here in honor of your great ancestry, I thought it would only be appropriate to bring this quest full circle by presenting you with your heirlooms, once again, while reliving the legacy that brought them here," he said, gesturing over to Colleen to begin.

"Ah, our lovely Megan. You are indeed a treasure to behold, that you are. You boldly took on this challenge to not only claim this here ring, but to discover your heart. It was your Granda's wish that you remembered who you really are: a writer, a romantic and a believer in true love.

"In opening yourself to the journey, and your heart to my dear Kieran, you have honored the *Legacy of Love Claddagh* ring, and it is with pride that I grant you its everlasting blessing," she said, placing the ring in Meg's hand and pulling her in for a tearful embrace.

"Mia Bella," Francesco began solemnly, saddened that he had to take our dear Sorella Maria's place. "Your cousin is looking down on you today as I present this cherished chest to you on her behalf. For you, this gift was destined to remind you that if you believe in yourself, anything is possible.

"As I look at you today, I see a transformed woman who has restored her faith in herself, and in her dreams. You will be an amazing restauranteur, but do not let that be the end of your passionate endeavors. As you take this hand carved jewelry box back into your possession, may it continue to inspire a lifelong pursuit of inner peace and happiness."

Mia proudly accepted her treasure, along with an affectionate kiss to the forehead, from a man I know she will hold dear to her heart for the rest of her life.

"And you, my firecracker of a cousin," EJ commenced,

"have finally come to the end of your personal mission. But before I hand this handsome devil over to you for good, I do believe I promised you a full history and symbolism.

"According to Iberian mythology, the dragon was a cave-dwelling, treasure-hoarding louse who imprisoned nymphs—kinda like Josh," he attempted to kid, but failed as we groaned and shook our heads.

"Too soon? My bad. Anyway, to be identified with a dragon in European culture was to be outcast as destructive, manipulative and evil. The only way to defeat such a force was to reflect its spell-casting eyes back at him with a shield.

"Now Goya, being a man of worldly intelligence, was equally enthralled with the east Asian philosophy that held the dragon in high reverence. They believed it symbolized inner strength, good fortune and the doorway to our intuitive guidance.

"So, when Goya designed his masterpiece, he wanted to blend the ancient Spanish mythology with the eastern world's more promising interpretation, as he believed both theories held truth. In creating the two heads, he wanted to represent the evil dragon that haunted him—his jealousy, greed and illicit sexuality. Something you might know a little bit about, huh honey?"

My cheeks reddened at his implication, but I assented with a shrug of the shoulders and a nod.

"The other head signified something much more formidable—his strength, valiance and pureness of heart. When he unleashed this side of him, it allowed his passions to turn to power instead of pain; prosperity instead of defeat.

"But in the end, he knew he had to embrace both sides

of him as one, with the understanding that whichever side decided to rear its head at any given moment was still worthy of his love and happiness. As I believe, sweet child, you have finally come to accept this within yourself."

"I have," I acknowledged.

"That being the case...Marissa Rossi, you have fulfilled your grandfather's dying decree that you live in harmony with both your strengths and your weaknesses, allowing them to catapult you into greatness. I hereby bestow upon you...oh wait.

"Before I do that," he said dramatically, taking the statue back before I could even touch it. "I have another story to tell."

"Now who's being a wicked dragon?" I goaded.

"Oh, I love how cheeky you are, cuz. But since you asked—how did the statue come to be in our family's possession? Fabulous question, Marissa.

"According to a letter that unfortunately has long since been lost and become hearsay, Goya was in love with a Rubio. Of course, to the world he was married to Josefa Bayeu and was thought to possibly have a young maiden lover somewhere along the way. But according to this letter—which I paraphrased in this little notebook for you so that you can remember the full story—she may not have been the only one to grace his bed.

"As I mentioned, he had first designed this dragon to represent the two parts of himself, but not just of good versus evil—of the one he presented to society and the one in his heart.

"When he fell in love with Marco Rubio, he had further embellished the statue with great riches for his paramour, the only man he said at the time knew the truth of his double-edged heart and yet accepted him for it with love.

"So although it was given for a forbidden love, the true meaning behind this legacy is to respect the duality of our souls and free ourselves from these societal chains that dictate we must be one or the other; when in fact, we all are both at our cores. It was then passed down to Marco's nephew, and years later down the line to the horrific Horace, his honorable son, Eduardo, and so on, finally leading to this moment.

"In the presentation of this rather magnificent creation to you, Marissa, it is done with the greatest pride and the deepest admiration. You have heroically and brazenly shown us the beauty of who you are, in every way, and we love you for it."

I lovingly removed the meaningful sculpture from his hands, granting him two cheek kisses before letting a few tears fall. His speech and profound words will live on in my heart forever.

"Now for the fun part," teased Colleen. "I reckon you'd all love to know what other secrets the ol' cod had in store for ya."

"Indeed," agreed EJ. "Now Marissa, did you happen to uncover the hidden map?"

"Well, somewhere in between me being held hostage and almost torched to death, I think I might have stumbled upon a clue," I mocked with sarcasm as he shook a naughty finger at me.

"I believe—" I said, giving the dragon's tail a mild twist to separate the tip from the body, "it is in here." Out came a small, weathered scroll tied with a thin blue ribbon.

"What does it say?" urged Meg. I opened it up as my two sisters gathered around me.

When three join as one
The seal can be undone
By fork in vine
The treasure be almost thine
By heart in center
You may finally enter

"Well, that's a riddle if I ever did hear one," murmured Mia. "I wonder what it means."

"When three join as one…must have to do with all three of these pieces, since Lena wouldn't have known about us as the three to go on this journey."

"Good call," approved Mia. "By fork in vine? I get the vine…that could be the ivy around the jewelry box. But what is the fork?"

It didn't take long for me to make the connection. "Oh! The tongues! The forked tongues of the dragon!" I exclaimed, excited to have a piece of the puzzle figured out so quickly.

"Heart in center…could it be the jewel of my ring, since it is shaped like a heart?" Meg offered.

"Boy, are you three smart, I reckon!" proclaimed Colleen.

"Yeah, but how does it all work to open this thing? There are no holes from what I can see," said Mia.

"Uh, how about you turn over that there piece of paper and look at the dang map?" teased EJ.

"Oh," I blushed, not considering that it could be two-sided. And there it was. An actual drawing of how all the pieces worked together to unlock the puzzle.

"Wow! I never would have figured this out, and I spent a lot of time examining that box," Mia professed.

"Leigh had quite the stir watching us trying to figure out this wretched box before he showed us the trick," confessed Colleen. "We didn't see the backside, neither."

"I can only imagine our grandfather's fun," I chuckled. "So, let's see the box. If we remove the tongues—forks—from the dragon's fire like this—ah, that was easy. No wonder they were wobbly. Glad I didn't get the chance to glue them in yet!" I handed over the two double-forked metal pieces to Mia.

"According to this diagram, they are supposed to be inserted into these tiny, little grooves hidden within the grapevine carving on both sides. Clever—so small that I missed them," said Mia, impressed over being so stumped.

Click, went the first key. *Clack,* went the second.

"In the spirit of full disclosure, those tongues are not actually part of the statue," EJ explained. "They were inserted later by Lena after she designed the puzzle box. Thought it was the best way to keep them safe."

"That actually makes a lot of sense," I responded. "I think we should keep it that way for now, until we know how our futures unfold. I'll arrange to have them placed more firmly so they don't fall out, though. So, what's next?"

"It looks like the stone of my ring is the other key—Kieran, are you able to remove this?"

He took the ring from Meg and examined it. With a small, delicate pop, it was released from its setting.

"We'll get it all nice and secure again when this is through," he promised her.

Mia then took the stone and placed it inside the center groove of the rose—another secret lock that none of us had seen before. With a press and turn of the gem and another unlocked sound, the top of the box snapped open.

"Holy crap, look at all that loot!" I couldn't believe the paperwork, jewelry and trinkets that filled the intricately carved wooden box. "What is all this?"

"I'm afraid we weren't privy to all the contents, *cara,*" said Francesco. "When we came together, Leigh explained his plan about each heirloom and how we all were to tell each story, and then showed us how the box opened. He shared nothing about what he intended to place inside.

"His grand scheme required a contract of silence on our part, which we eagerly signed. In return, to our surprise, he gifted us with a generous payment and a token of gratitude each. We all tried to refuse, but he would have none of it.

"It is a pity that none of you got to meet him—or that you didn't get to see him again," he addressed my mother and grandmother. "In the end, he really did want to do right by his family and shared his deep regrets with us. He wanted to be the man you fell in love with one last time."

Tears came to my grandmother's eyes but didn't dare to fall.

"It makes me happy to hear that," she said genuinely. "But there is something that I still don't understand about all of this. If he was forbidden to use any Marino money on our side of the family, how was he able to do all of this?"

"Ah, so Lena had an inheritance that Cian and Alessia had hidden in an Italian bank account set up by my father, the protection of which was passed down to me upon his death," Francesco continued. "Lena purposely never told her husband about it—it's how she was able to expense her overseas trips without being traced.

"Upon her death, she had it signed over to Leigh,

confiding about it when she disclosed these legacies. When we met up in Florence, he went down to *la banca* to arrange for Colleen, EJ and I—knowing that Sorella Maria would not be the best choice given her age, rest her soul—to take ownership of the account to fund your three trips and all expenses.

"Now that the quest is complete, we will be signing it over to the five of you women to withdraw and distribute however you see fit."

"How much is in there?" I couldn't help but ask.

"A whoppin' twenty mil!" hooted Colleen. "Well, give or take, since we did have to set up your little travel funds and whatnot."

"Twenty million dollars?" I thought my mother was going to pass out. *I* was going to pass out. Was this for real? What kind of scam was this?

"You can't be serious," Meg insisted.

"It's true, I've seen the ledger," EJ admitted. "Leigh had hoped that you would all dissolve the Italian account and each open your own in the States and begin your own legacy lines with it."

"Wow. Just wow. This is all so overwhelming," Granny said, needing to grab a chair and sit. Thankfully, Kieran was there to help her settle down.

"Now, don't get me wrong—I am extremely grateful for this gift. It just saddens me that what he leaves behind is money. I would have given anything in the world for him to turn his back on it and just be a family with us. To see him one final time. We lost so many years," she thought wistfully.

"Well, Granny, I intend to help a lot of people with this money," vowed Mia. "Maybe we'll never get the years back, but we can use this blessing to make other wrongs right in this world."

We all nodded in agreement; there would be no better tribute to our ancestors than to pay forward their kindness.

"So, if we were left these amazing treasures and all this money—what else could we possibly need from this box?" I asked.

"Might as well take a look," Meg suggested.

On the very top was an old white notecard with a blue rose. Within it was a folded up piece of paper that fell out to the ground. While Meg picked it up, Mia read the handwritten note inside the card.

Darling Leigh,

Always remember that you are just as much an O'Sullivan as you are a Marino. I am trusting you to honor our family legacies and find a way to keep the stories alive. Blessed be those who receive such rich keepsakes. I will be with you always.

Love, Mama

"How sweet."

"What does the letter say?" Meg unfolded the crinkled piece of paper to reveal a personal note from our grandfather wrapped around what appeared to be a computer USB.

My Final Legacy Letter

I thought you deserved to see me face-to-face as I revealed the final part of your lost legacy. I have recorded my last words to you on this drive. I only wish we could have met in person; I would have given anything to have hugged each of you at least once as

I said goodbye so that you could feel my love for you. So that I could leave this life with warmth. Perhaps in my next life, I will be a braver man. Beyond what I gift you now, I leave my heart and my pride with you, the beautiful family that you are.

With Love and Blessings Forevermore, Leigh Marino

"Does anyone have a laptop?" Meg asked. As if on cue, Francesco easily pulled one out of his leather briefcase and set us up so that we could watch the video Grandfather Leigh left for us.

As the screen faded from black to color, the image of our long-lost grandfather came into focus. Weathered and noticeably ill, we couldn't help but see the handsome face behind the wrinkles and the striking resemblance to each of us. We knew this man. We may never have met him, but we knew him.

Granny choked back a sob as the love of her life appeared before her on the screen. Her eyes wistfully gazed upon the kind aqua eyes of a man who had so much left to say, and no time to say it. Mom was less restrained in her tears, seeing her father for the last time. Protectively, Bruce brought her into a side embrace and held her with obvious love and respect to comfort her as she grieved once again.

With their blessing, we began his message.

Greetings my beloved family. I am Leigh Marino, son of Antonio Marino and Lena O'Sullivan. Ex-husband to the beautiful Lillith Mahoney; father to my diamond, Alissa Rossi; grandfather to Megan, Mia and Marissa Rossi; and grateful cousin and friend to Colleen O'Sullivan, Sorella Maria Bianchi, Francesco Marchesi and Edward John Rubio. This message is for all of you.

If you are watching this, it means my darling granddaughters have traveled to all three countries, met their wonderful cousins and successfully retrieved their inheritances. I am so proud of each of you—I hope that you found your journeys to be life-changing and more rewarding than you ever expected.

Now that these charms are in your possession, I must beg you to preserve our legacy and only pass them on to future generations who are worthy of the honor.

If your cousins have not yet revealed the Italian bank account, now would be the time to learn about it. It goes without saying, but to repay them for their kindness, I would hope that you would willingly present them with at least a million dollars each for their troubles.

We all looked at end other and nodded in agreement as our cousins started to protest. Even our virtual grandfather anticipated their resistance as he paused with a look as if to warn them not to object.

"We can argue about it later," Mia warned before gesturing for Francesco to resume playing the video.

But that is not the end of it, my dear family. Yes, there is more. It may seem like too much, but what else would a dying man do with the rest of his treasured possessions? These you are free to keep, sell or share as you'd like; only the ring, box and statue I request that you conceal and protect.

He stopped to gather his thoughts, a single tear escaping down his tarnished cheek. Seeing him like this made him real. His emotions, his gestures, his honesty. He became so much more than words on a piece of paper, and it moved us all. After a moment of silence, he began his words of farewell to each of us.

Mo shíorghrá Lillith,

In this box, you will find a few of our love letters and my most treasured photo of us. I looked at them daily, and though they may mean nothing to you at this point, I wanted you to have them. I hope that one day you can remember us fondly. You are the love of my life. Please remember that always.

I have also made arrangements with the matriculation office at Pace University to enroll you and have your tuition paid in full. It is one promise I can finally keep to you. My dear, it is never too late to fulfill your dreams. Go get that criminal justice degree you always wanted and fight for those underdogs. The world is a better place because you are in it. I know mine was.

I loved you. When I met you. When I married you. When I left you. And now, as I die. I will take my love for you into my eternal grave.

His words ended with shaky hands that blew a kiss through the screen as he mouthed "I love you" once more. Equally shaken, Granny gestured to the man on the screen with her own kiss goodbye and words of gratitude and love.

My little diamond, Alissa,

I have also left you quite a few photos of us, along with the card you had made me for my birthday the first year I left. I treasured everything about you. You will also find a rare, original edition of your favorite childhood book, "I Will Love You Forever." Because that, I will.

He then proceeded to read a few lines from the book, moving my mother to deeper tears and a hidden smile—her last memory of him can now be a happy one. No longer will it be the moment he left; it will be his recitation of a book she held dear to her heart. He continued his message to her, though we all struggled with the poignancy of his video. Not a dry eye sat on that rooftop.

If I am correct, you have not yet visited the refurbished home I set up for you and your mother. I know it must hold many painful memories and I cannot blame you for hesitating. However, I ask that you go at least once. There is something more I added to it for you—a new wing that serves as an Elizabethan Library, fully stocked with every book, novel, play and poem from every era you can imagine. There is also a classroom; share your passion with children and keep the love of the classics alive. Teach them and start a new generation of literature lovers.

There is nothing I would love more than to see your wisdom spark a revolution—except to see you fall in love again. Open your heart, sweet diamond. As I wished nothing but a happy future for my Lillith, I know Joseph would have wished the same for his beloved. Your heart is too good and too pure to go unshared. But I shall warn you—if you find a devil like me, I will use my heavenly superpowers to punch his lights out.

It was a much-needed joke to lighten up the crowd, before Grandfather Leigh signed off with his last words of love for his little girl. Bruce fondly looked at my mother, who kissed him gently and assured him that her father would most certainly not be coming after him. After all the times I misjudged him, I could finally see he was the perfect man for her. I gave him a wink of approval to let him know he had my blessing as well.

Video resuming, we knew it would be our turn. With such extraordinary heirlooms in our possession and a multi-million dollar account, I couldn't imagine what else he could possibly want to give us.

My bold Megan,

I have a feeling that Ireland will call to you, and as such, Colleen and I have already arranged to turn the deed to the O'Sullivan family home over to you. It will now be yours: live it in, visit it, turn it into a home exchange or timeshare for the rest of the family or sell it—the choice is yours.

My only request of you going forward is that you write and publish our story (as fiction, of course) and embrace the author inside you. Let your words speak your truth. If there is anything I can share from my life's mistakes, it's that love is much more important than power. Find it and hold on to it.

A kiss from Kieran sealed that deal.

My sweet Mia,

I hope you have discovered that happiness is more than serving others; it is also honoring your own dreams. That being said, I have purchased for you a beautiful abandoned building in a prime location along the water for your restaurant. If you do not like it, you are free to sell it and invest elsewhere, of course.

In an envelope is a list of contractors I have already vetted for you—good, honest workers who can oversee the entire construction of your dream. Do me a favor, please. Even though

I am sure you will offer much more sophisticated cuisine, can you always keep your grandmother's sausage and peppers on the menu? It is my favorite, and no other recipe has ever come close. And don't let this be the end of your dreams—always keep believing in whatever your heart desires.

Mia laughed as she promised the man on the screen that she would wrangle the recipe out of Granny's hands somehow. Granny, of course, lovingly teased Mia that she'd leave it to her in her own will. What a wicked sense of humor my grandmother sometimes had.

I took a deep breath in, wondering what was in store for me.

My fiery Marissa,

I have never seen your work, but I have witnessed your passion. I have no doubt that you have a successful career ahead of you. And every artist deserves a proper studio and gallery to exhibit her artwork.

That's why my final gift to you is the purchase of the Rubio Art Gallery. I have other plans for EJ and Rodney, and the transfer of the deed shall be complete upon your viewing of this video. It will be your space, and your cousin has promised to mentor you along the way. Never stop creating from your heart. And always keep an eye out for those struggling artists like yourself; give them the chance to shine as you have been given. Everyone deserves to express themselves and be accepted for who they are, as do you. Never forget your perfection.

"EJ, you knew about this?" I asked incredulously.

"Mmm-hmm. Now hush and let the man speak," he warned playfully. Grandfather Leigh concluded with addressing each of his trusted cousins.

Darling Colleen,

Words cannot express my gratitude for all you have done for me and our family. There is not much I can give you, except this: your dream of traveling around the world. Enclosed is an envelope with travel agent information; they have the plans lined up for a cruise around Alaska, a spiritual retreat in Bali and a vay-cay on the sunny shores of Fiji. They just need dates that you can go and any companion of your choice—perhaps your cousin Mary? Enjoy seeing the world. And thank you from the bottom of my heart.

Dearest Sorella Maria,

I know your vows forbid you from extravagant gifts. However, in gratitude, it is my wish for you to have this treasured ivory angel statue and rosary my mother prayed with daily. I know your cousin would want you to have them. You are a blessing, and I humbly thank you. It was an honor to have spent time with you listening to your stories. I am forever changed by your wisdom.

Francesco,

My deepest appreciation to you for your discretion and support. I could not have done this without your guidance and resources. I have one final favor to ask of you. As Sorella Maria cannot accept grand gestures, I am hoping you will accept this gift on her behalf.

Her old convent, now a hotel, will be undergoing renovations upon your presentation of the enclosed contract. The owner was looking to retire, and I have set him up handsomely. The intention is to convert this building into a home for single mothers and abused women who have been turned away from their families, in honor of Concetta and Maria's struggle—The Maria Bianchi Women's Center.

Though I must admit, it is also in acknowledgment of how I left my beloved Lillith and Alissa behind to suffer on their own. I cannot make it up to them, but I can help others who were equally abandoned in retribution.

All plans are set; all I ask of you is to oversee that my wishes are carried out and that you accept ownership of the deed. To thank you and your brother for your kindness, a wing is being built in the Marchesi name. May your legacy live on as ours does.

My American cousins EJ and Rodney,

You light up my life with your kind hearts and generosity. I know you think it is too late to raise your own children, and I respect your wishes—but I have a greater plan for you. As you retire from the art community, it is my wish that you find purpose in my final project—a new Rubio Community Center for foster children. Although you will not have any children of your own, there is nothing stopping you from caring for those without a family and filling that void in your life and in theirs. Give them the love and guidance they deserve and I promise the love you get back will astound you.

The three cousins just stared out in reverence for a

man they actually had the pleasure of meeting. None of us wanted the video to end; it felt so cruel to finally see the man behind the letters, to get to know our grandfather on sight, for it to just end like this forever. But this was all we had, and we needed to cherish what little bit of him we did get to hold on to as he left us with parting words.

And now I may rest in peace, knowing I have taken care of my loved ones and attempted to make a difference to those who suffer through my death. While I have learned that money will never buy happiness, my wish is that you use the resources at your disposal to follow your hearts, do some good in this world and always, always remember that family and love come first.

I love you all. Thank you for allowing me the chance to right my wrongs. I promise to love and protect you from above.

"This is unbelievable," murmured Francesco, finally breaking the revered silence. "I am so honored to be a part of this, and I know Sorella Maria was, too. I will take the angel and rosary and lay them on her grave, so that they will be with her forever. And I will make sure that shelter helps hundreds of families."

Mia grabbed his hand in gratitude. "Thank you, Francesco. For everything. I'm inspired to build a sister center in the heart of New York. Perhaps you can help guide me with another dream." He looked at my big-hearted sister and simply kissed her and replied with an "of course."

"I can't believe I'm going around the world," said Colleen in a rare moment of speechlessness. "Bless his soul."

"I can't believe we are going to have a family like we always wanted to," said Rodney, hugging his love. "I never considered fostering as an option. Think of all the kids we can help and love," he beamed as EJ sentimentally kissed his husband in great joy.

"And I'm getting your art gallery. I don't know what to say, EJ."

"There's nothing to say. I'm leaving it in great hands, and I couldn't be more tickled to move on to a new chapter in my life. On that note, I have something to show you."

He brought us over to the right side of the rooftop, where a glass top table stood with three easels and golden leaf title cards displaying my paintings: *Fire Resistant, Shadow of the Sun* and *Pleasure Conundrum.*

"You remembered," I said, astonished that EJ recalled the names I had lovingly given them during our conversation in the studio.

"Honey, these are wonderful," my Mom said with pride.

"This is how it will look in three weeks when I add them to my Fall exhibition—before we transition the gallery over to you," EJ announced with honor and commitment. "Although, they will be hanging on a wall and not on a table."

"I'm so proud of you," proclaimed Granny. "I told you this would happen. I knew once you let your heart do the work, you'd become the artist you were always meant to be."

"Thanks, Granny. I think each of us got exactly what we wanted—even if we didn't know what that was," I said, looking at my two sisters and taking each of their hands and sending a wink to Jay.

"That's for certain," Mia agreed, smiling big at

Francesco, the man who opened the door to loving herself. "I had an appointment with a real estate agent next week to find the best place for my restaurant, but I think I'll check out my new building first.

"I'll have to look into these contractors and make sure they align with my vision, but if all goes well, I can start construction in a few weeks and have a grand opening in the spring. I would love for you all to be there. If I send you an invitation, will you come?"

"Will the meal be free?" EJ joked. "I'm just joshin' ya—of course we will be there, honey!"

"You can count on it," smiled Francesco. "And perhaps we can use the real estate agent for your new family center while I am there."

Colleen gave a big thumbs up as I threw table confetti into the air in congratulations.

"It's so unreal that this is finally going to happen," Mia reflected. "In a weird way, I feel like life is finally where I've always wanted it to be. I have a great family, amazing kids and now a dream come true. What else could a girl ask for?"

"It certainly is a gift," Granny agreed. "I'm still in shock that he fulfilled his promise to send me to college. I'm going to finally get my degree," she said giddily like a little girl.

"And I can't wait to explore my new library," Mom added. "I know it might be hard at first, Mama, but I think I am ready to forgive and move on. Yes, what Daddy set up for all of us was built from his fortune. But all the good he is putting in place eases my personal pain of abandonment. Think of all the families and children we can teach, help and heal because of his generosity. It's comforting to know that after everything, the heart you fell in love with—that created all of us—is who he chose to be in the end."

"I couldn't have said it better myself, my sweet girl," agreed Granny. "It is time to put the anger and resentment behind us and start living again. To remember who we are and to use our gifts to make a difference in this world. Time to create new life."

Catching a glance at Meg and Kieran staring into each other's eyes and suppressing a giggle like they had a secret, I prompted them to speak.

"What's up with you two?" I asked as Kieran nodded at his beloved.

"Well, we were going to wait until after the party to tell everyone, but since everyone is here…" She lifted up her left hand to uncover a stunning princess cut diamond ring. The boy had some taste!

"You're getting married?" Mia screamed in excitement. "When?"

"Well, we're thinking by Christmas," Kieran responded. "A small, intimate wedding in Ireland where my mum can be there and then a bigger reception later in the summer in New York."

"Why so soon and spread out?" asked Mom curiously.

"Well, like Granny said, it's time to create new life. Looks like I'm ahead of the game–because I'm pregnant," Meg answered shyly to shouts of excitement and well wishes. "We just found out last week. It explains why I've been so tired this trip."

"How wonderful for y'all! So, how will this all work with the across-the-ocean thing?" EJ asked, addressing the obvious.

"The plan is to live in the States September through June—the school year, essentially. Then, we figured we'd live in Ireland during the summers and go back as often as we can to visit Kieran's mum with the baby."

"Sounds like a great plan," Mom supported.

"This is absolutely amazing. To be here with all of you like this, and so happy," I teared up, never so content in my entire life. "I never want to forget this night."

"I think we should have a reunion every year," suggested Mia.

"Yes! What a splendid idea! Absolutely!" cheered the rest of the group.

"Shall we have one final toast?" Jay prodded, and we all gestured for him to lead the way.

"To five incredible women, who I have known and loved my whole life. And to their extended family of generous, kind cousins who have made their lives complete. May you all always have the love and joy you have now and be blessed for the rest of your days."

"Cheers! Here, here!" came the group shouts and clinking glasses. With the final reveal at its conclusion, our tormentor behind bars and no more mysteries to solve, we were all free to eat, drink and be merry. As I stood looking at my art with great pride and hope for the future, I felt Jay come up behind me and wrap his arms around my waist, putting his head on my shoulder.

"So, how does it feel to finally get everything you ever wanted?"

"It's more than I ever expected. I never thought I would see a day like this. I mean, look around. I'm at a family gathering and I finally feel like I belong instead of being the black sheep. And yet, nothing has changed except the way I react. There's no jealousy, no resentment—just genuine love for everyone here.

"And I look at these canvases—these rather dark

visions I created, and am amazed at how accepted they are, just as they are. How accepted *I* am. I feel—free."

"I, for one, would change nothing about you. I'm glad to hear that you finally feel the same way about yourself."

"I do. The only demon I had to face was my self-judgment. That part of the dragon is now gone, and I'm ready to let the bright one lead the way."

"I hope that other dragon is not *all* gone," he said suggestively, with a slight smirk on his face as he turned me around to face him.

"Oh no, not all of it," I swore with my own alluring look. "There are parts of me that will never change. You can count on that, lover."

I leaned up to kiss him passionately with the promise of forever, knowing that with Jay, I can be both the dark and the light. And there is no other way I would ever want to be.

Rubio Family Line

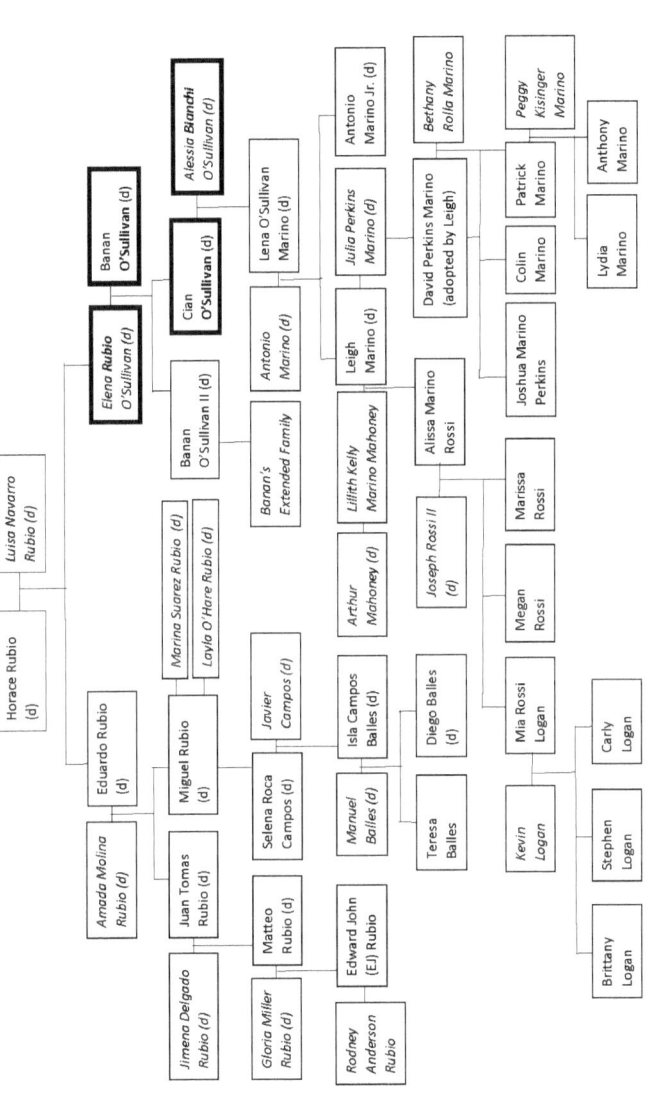

Other Books by Jenny Dee

The Lost Heritage Trilogy

Call of the Celts
A Tuscan Treasure
The Catalan Key

Autobiographical Memoirs

Butterfly Travels
Butterfly Travels 2

The Cosmic Kids Club Series

Meet the Z Team
Planet Personalities
Stars Live in Houses, Too
Cosmic Kids Astrology

About Jenny Dee

An avid writer since childhood, my career in professional writing anchored my passion and encouraged my dream to become an author—my first book, *Butterfly Travels,* was published in 2014. Five years later, my children joined me in both my physical and literary journeys, and we are delighted to share our family adventures with the world through *Butterfly Travels 2.*

I've never been a "one size fits all" type of girl. I like to connect to all kinds of people and share my stories and experiences in hopes that they touch a life. I don't ever want my inspiration to be limited to a single genre, so it is with a great love for writing that I offer a multitude of styles to strike your fancy, from travel memoirs and children's books to empowered women's literature and romance.

To learn more about me or to subscribe to my publications, you can find me at <u>www.jennydeeauthor.com</u> or simply scan this QR code.

~ Find Yourself in a Character ~

www.ingramcontent.com/pod-product-compliance
Lightning Source LLC
Chambersburg PA
CBHW071605110726
47908CB00007B/2249